EPISODES OF VIOLENCE

DAVID BERNSTEIN

PRAISE FOR EPISODES OF VIOLENCE

DAVID BERNSTEIN

"This story was fast-paced and gritty, a call-back to our younger days, and the lack of remorse we thrived on at that age. Violence, destruction, and chaos have never been so beautifully woven into a story that so many of us can relate to. I loved it! The antithesis of chaos, violence, and the remorselessness of those who inflict it."
— Stuart Bray, author of VIOLENCE ON THE MEEK

Contents

PART 1: PATH OF DESTRUCTION

Chapter One

The barn-shaped mailbox exploded as the baseball bat smashed through it. Various-sized jagged pieces of red plastic scattered into the air, a few pinging off the hockey mask Jade was wearing.

"That's a fucking ten," she yelled as refreshing summer wind roughly caressed her body while she hung halfway out of the Camry's window.

Looking out through the rear window, Bobby said, "That's an eight."

Jade slid back inside the vehicle and plopped down onto the passenger seat, the bat between her knees. "Fuck off. That was a ten. Nine at the worst."

"You left a quarter of the mailbox."

"Bullshit," Jade said and pulled up the hockey mask so it rested on top of her head. She then grabbed her can of beer from the cup holder, popped the top and sent a spritz of foam onto the dash and a dribble onto her perky chest. Without wasting a second, the can was at her lips, her throat muscles working feverishly as she guzzled. A few moments later, she let loose a loud burp and then tossed the empty can out the window, pulled the mask back down and climbed back outside, taking the bat with her.

The rush of night air threatened to steal her weapon. She held it firmly. Her purple-colored hair was yanked back, the strands whipping about like tentacles. Exhilaration filled her and the only other time she felt as good was when Daemon was making her come. The Camry's four-cylinder engine whined as her lover stomped the gas pedal.

"Come on, babe," Daemon said from the driver's seat.

The car moved closer to the side of the backwoods road as another mailbox approached. Jade felt the vehicle slow and knew her boyfriend was trying to give her a better shot at blasting her next target. *Fuck.* She loved him more than he could know. Would drink his piss and chew his shit if it meant saving him from death. But they were playing a game. Everyone was out for themselves. She didn't want favoritism just because she sucked his cock and fucked him. "Don't you dare slow down, assface," she yelled, and a second later felt the wind pick up. She could play with the males just fine.

With the bat in hand, her muscles straining a bit against the wind, she was in her stance. The next mailbox was a replica barn with white trim and a white X across the front door. *How fucking cute*, she thought, salivating at not only destroying it, but thinking about how upset the stupid owner would be when he saw it.

It was a big sucker too. She'd need to hit it square and well, or a lot of it would remain on the pole. Points would be lost, and she'd have to hear Bobby's mouth—not that they kept a true log like some damn bowling league. The points were just mailbox to mailbox.

Her grip tightened as she choked up on the bat. With a grunting effort, she swung. The baseball-hitting tool collided into the side of the mailbox. The wooden container burst apart as if made of bamboo, the material much more delicate than Jade had anticipated.

Glancing back as the car sped away, she saw that she'd gotten it all. There was nothing left standing but the metal pole. She pumped her fist into the air before slipping back into the car.

"No fucking doubt about that one," she said and pulled off the mask.

"Yeah, yeah," Bobby said, matter-of-factly.

"Hand the lady a cold one man," Daemon said. "That was some shot."

Bobby reached into the ice-filled cooler that was on the floor behind the driver's seat, withdrew a can of beer and handed it to a grinning Jade. She opened it and clanked beers with Daemon.

It was stupid to drink and drive, especially while performing an illegal activity such as mailbox baseball. But for the most part, there was no arguing and winning with Daemon. The young man did what he wanted to do when he wanted to do it.

Daemon finished his beer in a few gulps and tossed the empty can out the window. It was his second since they had started the game, but his sixth within the last two hours. Bobby couldn't help but keep a record of such things.

"Damn, I feel good," Daemon said and howled out the window.

"C'mon, Jade," Bobby said. "You've got one more turn, then I'm up. We already passed two mailboxes while you idiots celebrated. We haven't been on this road in a few weeks and won't be able to come back for a while. So, let's take advantage and get as many as we can."

Jade laughed and told him to fuck himself.

"You really are the queen of fuck, you know that?" Bobby said.

"Fuck yeah I do," Jade said, pulled the hockey mask down and climbed out the window.

Another mailbox was coming into view. It was a boring-looking piece of square ugliness, a simple gray in color. Jade preferred smashing pretty ones, ones that homeowners thought would look so damn cute in front of their house as they held hands and walked down the aisle of the store where they purchased it. Even better were the mailboxes people constructed themselves. They put all that hard work into it, only to see it destroyed.

Jade didn't fully understand why she loved hurting other people. Some individuals enjoyed golf or movies or collecting things. She liked to ruin stuff and watch people's happiness dwindle. There was nothing anyone could do about it either except to gather up the broken pieces, throw them in the trash and put up another mailbox and hope the hooligans wouldn't return.

But she and her friends did come back. They'd been doing so in irregular fashion so as not to set a pattern and to give false hope that the vandals had moved on—that it had been a one-time thing. They were a reckless bunch and quite daring with what they did—mailbox baseball, flattening police cars' tires and shoplifting everything from car parts to beer despite not needing to do so on account of Bobby's wealth. They were smart with how they went about it. Bobby was a brainiac, and Jade, for as much as she teased him, liked Bobby most of the time. He was the little brother, despite his being a foot and a half taller than her, she never had.

It had only been three weeks since the last time they'd played the game on Hickamore Street. But the group was feeling good from all the weed and booze they'd ingested and really wanted to bash the wealthier homes' mailboxes. The rich folk had the best ones.

Within striking distance, Jade swung the bat. The mailbox gave, bending inward, but didn't break. The bat seemed to stick to it and was ripped from her grasp, her wrists painfully bending backward. "Fuck," she cried out as the bat tumbled along the side of the road, the mailbox unharmed.

The container was made of rubber. Soft, pliable rubber.

Headlights came to life in the house's driveway and a black SUV tore down it and onto the road, the tires screeching. The truck's engine sounded mean, and Jade imagined a pissed off dude behind the wheel with his foot pinning the gas pedal to the floor. The driver quickly caught up to them. Blinded by the bright lights both above and below the grill, Jade slipped back into the car.

"We've got a problem," she said.

"You don't say," Bobby said, staring out the back window.

"What the hell happened back there?" Daemon asked and hit the black button under the steering wheel column that caused the 007-like contraption that Bobby made to go into effect, dropping the stolen Pennsylvania license plates over the registered New York ones.

"Fucking rubber mailbox," Jade said. "And if that wasn't bad enough, we got a Waiter."

"Man, I hate Waiters," Daemon said, and slammed the steering wheel with his fist.

"Yeah, it's like they have no lives," Jade said. "Wasting all their time waiting around for us to come back so they can catch us. And for what, ruining a fifty-dollar piece of trash?"

"Well, this motherfucker was waiting and I'm sure he's pissed," Bobby said. "And most of the mailboxes on this road are in the hundreds of dollars. He's probably been sitting in his driveway every night for three weeks, salivating like a rabid dog."

"Good," Daemon said. "Glad we could give the fucker something to do and make him waste his time."

"Won't be wasting his time if he catches us," Bobby said.

Despite the glaring beams of the SUV, Daemon looked at the rearview mirror and caught Bobby's stare, freezing him.

"He ain't catching nothing but the shit we give him," Daemon said. "You hear?"

"Yeah, this ain't our first rodeo," Jade said. "Sometimes I think you're a big pussy, Bobby."

"I am what I eat," Bobby said.

Besides the gadget license plate that Bobby installed in the event of being chased, the vehicle was always spray-painted with Plasti Dip, a rubberized coating that was easily removable. Anyone looking for a certain color Toyota Camry with Pennsylvania license plates would never find it. After a night of mailbox baseball, the car was stripped of its coating and put back to its original faded evergreen color.

The car looked average—which was perfect—with a few scratches and minor dents, but the engine was kept up well by Daemon who worked as a mechanic. The car could move when it needed to.

But the vehicle chasing them was a V-8 monster, its engine heard over all else. It could easily stay with them and run them off the road should the driver be as unstable as the trio in the Camry. And if the SUV's driver had called the cops, that meant more trouble.

But the delinquents had prepared for such contingencies.

"Bobby," Daemon said as the SUV came within an inch of the bumper, "I think it's time you do your thing."

Bobby turned around and yanked down the other half of the back seat, headrest and all. With a clear passageway into the trunk, he crawled inside and hit the light switch that he'd installed. The small compartment lit up, giving him a clear view of the mostly empty space, which included shooter's headphones, a box of ammo and the 12-gauge shotgun that rested in a black leather bag.

Unzipping the bag, he took hold of the weapon and loaded it with buckshot. The car swerved, and he dropped the last shell. As it attempted to roll away, he reached out and snatched it up before quickly depositing it into the gun. He didn't think he'd need all the shells, never had, but it was always good to be thorough. Once the shooting started, anything could happen.

Bobby put on the sound-dampening headphones, turned the trunk light off, then crawled to the back of the trunk and slid open the gun-slit he'd made. Bright light poured in, making it difficult to see anything. Squinting, he cocked the gun and poked the barrel through the slit and did his best to aim for the pursuing vehicle's front tire.

He pulled the trigger.

The 12-gauge rammed into his shoulder, the sound dull to his ears thanks to the headphones. His muscles and bones absorbed the kick, his body conditioned to shooting powerful firearms. The SUV's right headlight was blown out. The vehicle swerved, the tires screeching.

With the remaining headlight no longer directly on him, Bobby was able to see the truck's front tire. It was huge and inviting. He angled the gun and fired. The heavily treaded tire burst as the buckshot tore through it. The truck tipped forward and to the side. Sparks flew as the chrome bumper scraped along the pavement. The 4x4's back end lifted off the ground as the truck went into a tumble. Glass shattered and metal crunched, bits of car flinging everywhere until it met a thick oak where it stopped cold.

Bobby kept an eye on the wreckage until the road dipped and he lost sight of it. Dropping the shotgun, he tore off the headphones and scurried into the back seat. "Did you guys see that?"

"Holy shit, yeah," Daemon said and punched the roof.

"That was badass," Jade said and held up her hand for Bobby to high-five it.

Bobby was a little numb. His feelings about what had just happened were not at the forefront of his mind. Wanting to go with the situation, he moved to high-five Jade when she pulled her hand away and said, "Sucker."

He'd fired on vehicles before. Two, in fact. The first Waiter that had chased them had backed off after he fired a warning shot. The second car hadn't taken the hint, so he'd been forced to shoot at it, putting a hole in its grill. He had always supposed someone could wind up getting hurt, with the probability increasing every time they went out, but never focused on it for too long.

Seeing his friends celebrate with cheers and hand claps made him feel like he was missing out on something great. He wanted to be happy, too. There was nothing to stop him. It wasn't like he knew the driver or was going to get caught—he'd made sure of that by hooking up the license plate gadget and the gun slit for the sole purpose of getting away clean.

His thoughtfulness and planning had paid off. He smiled at the thought. At his work proving itself. He was like a villain in a movie. A supervillain. Suddenly, he grew warm inside and joined in the celebration by grabbing a beer and saying. "Fuck yeah, that was awesome." This brought being bad to a whole new level.

Jade was all over Daemon, her tongue sliding up the side of his neck, her hand on his crotch. "I'm so fucking hot right now."

"Calm down, babe," Daemon said. "I'll take care of you later. We got company."

"Let him watch," she said. "I don't care." She glanced at Bobby and laughed, then sat back in her seat. She held out her hand again toward Bobby, indicating for him to slap it. When he didn't move, she said, "Seriously, man. That was some badass shooting, Bobby." She kept her hand out and motioned with it for him to high-five her. "C'mon, man, give me some sweetness."

Not wanting to miss her hand, he shot it out as fast as possible and practically punched her palm.

"I wasn't going to pull it away, assfucker."

"Just making sure."

"Hand me another beer, bartender," she said.

Bobby plucked one from the cooler, the ice still intact, and handed it to her.

"What am I, fucking invisible?" Daemon asked.

"Yeah, bartender," Jade said. "Hand the man a brewsky."

When I'm up to bat, you'll be the beer-bitch—remember that," Bobby said and tossed her a beer that she popped open and handed to Daemon.

"Stop the car," Jade yelled.

Daemon kept driving.

"I said stop the fucking car."

"No, you didn't," Bobby said. "You said stop the car. Not stop the fucking car."

"Eat me."

"What's the problem, babe?" Daemon asked and caressed Jade's cheek.

"I want to go back and take pictures," she said, lips pursed, arms crossed over her chest.

"I kind of want to too," Bobby said, feeling his stomach drop. He wasn't sure if it was morbid or just to see the result of his actions. Not seeing what he'd caused was like only reading half the story. He had to know how it turned out, despite it being a terrible idea.

"Fuck that guy," Daemon said and upended his beer can. His Adam's apple bobbed up and down as he swallowed. Finished, he crushed the can in his hand and tossed it out the window. "I hope that asshole's SUV is totaled. Fuck it, I hope he's dead."

"You think the driver's dead?" Jade asked, mouth hanging open.

Bobby swallowed, feeling a small lump in his throat. Dead? He didn't think that was the case. It wasn't that he cared about the driver. He didn't. But a death would mean a more serious police presence. The scene combed over.

It was odd not caring if the person was dead or alive. If they went back and the driver was dying, he would have the power to possibly save him—or let him die. That much power over another person was intense, the feeling new and worth exploring. It was getting caught and going to prison that frightened him. He wasn't cut out for that life. Daemon and Jade were loose cannons and crazy. They would survive incarceration. That was the problem with smarter people. They thought about the future. People like Daemon and Jade lived in the present. He envied them for that.

It was freeing not to give a shit if the person lived or died. It meant he had no guilt. In fact, he never had guilt about much. No one cared about him, so why should he care about some stranger? A faceless asshole who thought he was some kind of vigilante.

His parents cared, or at least pretended to. Like when they watched the news and saw a report about some fuckhead mother who'd left her kids in a car on a ninety-degree day with the windows open an inch, as if that would make a difference, and the kids died. Or when those commercials came on about starving kids in other countries, their skeletal-like frames and grotesque pot bellies. His parents would say how bad they felt and how they wished the world was a better place for everyone.

The unnerving thing was, when they spoke about such things, Bobby saw nothing in their eyes. No compassion or yearning. They never donated to any causes, despite their wealth. It was like they were putting on an act when they were in front of him, hoping their words would come across the right way and teach him how people were supposed to feel.

They were fucking liars.

Cold, like him.

The truth was, they didn't care about him anymore than they cared about each other. So how were strangers supposed to care about him? Had anyone given a shit when he was getting beat up in the Shop Rite parking lot? People recorded it on their phones and others called 911, but no one intervened. Or when he fell on his skateboard and was bloodied up. No one wanted to come too close. People only said things like, "Are you okay" and "you should be more careful" and "you need to wear a helmet and knee and elbow pads."

For the first time in his life, he wasn't mad at those people. Those uncaring assholes, because he was one, too.

"Can't we go back, please?" Jade asked.

"It isn't a good idea," Bobby said. "The cops might be on their way. Another motorist might have stopped. People might have heard the crash and are coming out of their houses, despite the acres of woodland between houses."

"You heard the man," Daemon said. "No way we take a chance."

Jade threw her arms up. "Oh well, I tried. Maybe next time."

"Guess this neighborhood is off limits for quite a while now," Daemon said, lighting a cigarette.

"Yeah," Bobby said. "For at least six months."

"So where to now?" Jade asked. "I'm still up."

"No, you're not," Bobby said. "That last one counted. You got zero points."

"Fuck off," Jade said, giving him the finger.

"Sorry, babe," Daemon said, exhaling a lungful of smoke. "He's right."

Jade shoved him. "Maybe he can suck your dick tonight, then."

"We'll head over to the other side of town," Daemon said. "Hit Maple Street. It's been a while, I think."

"Yeah," Jade said, jumping in her seat with excitement. "About time we hit Brewmeyer again, that prick fuck."

Daemon flung his cigarette butt out the window and as he exhaled said, "Worst teacher in history. Man's got it coming and more."

"And I get to do it this time," Bobby said, rubbing his hands together like some evil cartoon villain.

"Lucky bastard," Jade said.

Daemon stayed on the back roads and made it to Maple Street in fifteen minutes, driving the speed limit. Since they had begun their mailbox baseball routine a year ago, the cops had supposedly amped up their investigation into the property damaging bandits, but in a small town with a five-person police force there wasn't much to be done without catching them in the act or hearing something via word-of-mouth. The crime wasn't worth calling in the State Troopers. This was a good thing, but it also pissed off Daemon.

Mailbox baseball was kid's stuff, an activity high school teens took part in. Sure, it had been fun for a while, but now it was growing old. He wanted something else, something that would give him more of a rush and cause more chaos. Jade still seemed to get off on it, but the girl was nuts and got off on almost anything destructive.

Getting pursued by Waiters was something he enjoyed. The thrill of the chase, as the saying went. It was true. If only he had a better, faster car. The latest chase had been phenomenal. He wished he could've relived it. They might have to add a video camera to their mailbox baseball supplies, despite Bobby saying such things were bad for business and always got people in trouble. But what he really wanted was to do something that wouldn't be forgotten. Something that would horrify the town and baffle the law.

However, this last encounter with a Waiter would most likely prove serious enough to push the mailbox baseballers up on the cops' most wanted list. They had used firearms before, but now that they added vehicular damage, serious injuries, and possibly death...

The more he thought about it, the more he wished he'd gone back and seen the wreckage. He'd love to whip out his penis and piss all over the driver. Then he'd take the bat, break the guy's legs and skull. Thinking about the violence got him semi-hard.

Looking at Jade, he wanted her right then and there. Tell Bobby to wait outside while he banged the shit out of her. But even more than that, he wanted to hurt someone. Use his hands up close. Cause real harm. Change a person's life because they fucked with him or were simply in the wrong place at the wrong time. Just walk up to a person, male or female, and clock them cold. Make someone fear the unknown and be afraid to walk down the street.

"What's wrong, babe?" Jade asked.

"Nothing."

"Bullshit," Jade said, then tickled him under his chin. "Coochie, coochie—"

Daemon swatted her hand away.

Jade giggled. "Poor baby. What's wrong?"

He hated coochie, coochie coo, and Jade knew it. She could be such a bitch at times. He'd told her how his low-life mother used to do it when he was younger, before Eugene entered their lives and turned his mother into a junkie.

CHAPTER TWO

Shortly after Daemon's twelfth birthday, his father ran out on him and his mother, causing her to spiral in and out of depression. Her sister came and helped out around the house while his mother received help from a psychologist. With medication, his mother improved a little and got a new job, one that would allow her to keep the house. Before then, it had been Daemon's father who made a good portion of the household's money. Daemon's mother had been doing what she loved, painting and selling her art over the internet and at local arts and crafts fairs.

Daemon had always imagined he'd see the man again, that his father would one day walk through the front door and beg his mother for forgiveness. He tried looking for the man, but to no avail. His mother wanted nothing to do with the son-of-a-bitch, and if he returned, she'd kick his ass right back out. She would make it on her own.

As weeks turned into months, and there was no sign of his father, Daemon gave up hope that he'd ever see him again. Then two years later, they were informed that the man had died in a car accident. Death benefits were going to his new family. Daemon's father had changed his name within weeks of leaving him and his mom, which was the reason Daemon hadn't been able to locate him. The man had given his wife instructions that, in the event of his death; she was to inform his ex-family. She certainly didn't have to after the fact but did as he had wanted out of her love for him. It didn't make sense that the asshole wanted nothing to do with Daemon and his mom, but made sure they knew when he died.

The news sent his mother into a tailspin; the past roaring up in force. Daemon had been shaken too. There was no explanation as to why his father left. Had it been something he'd done? Something his mother had done? Was his father just a bastard? Had his father just fallen in love with another woman? Did his father love him? Hate him? In the end, Daemon figured it was simply another way to hurt them.

He wrote to his father's second wife and asked all the questions that ran through his mind, but never received a reply. He felt somewhat hollow inside, as if a piece of his soul had been taken or killed. So, he turned to his mother for guidance and everything else a mother was supposed to be. She was a wreck, but she was all he had.

Eventually, his mother wound up losing her job, her boss stating she'd taken too many days off and wasn't reliable. She doubled up on her assortment of mood stabilizers and depression medication, and when her insurance lapsed, she turned to booze. Frequenting the dive known as the Purple Pony, she met Eugene, the scumbag who'd introduced her to a plethora of narcotics, including heroin and cocaine.

Unable to make mortgage payments, Daemon's mother was in jeopardy of losing the house, and that's when Eugene moved in. He was a total loser; ten years older than his mom, ugly with a crooked nose, balding head, a face deeply scarred with pockmarks and most of all, a complete jerk. He oozed vileness, like some slimy creature with beady eyes and fangs that crawled out of the gutter and sought ways to steal people's souls.

Daemon came home from school numerous times to find his mom and Eugene screwing in the living room, kitchen or their bedroom with the door wide open—even twice in his room. After catching them the second time, he stole a lock from the local hardware store and secured his room. There were other times he'd find them passed out somewhere in the house, clothed or naked, with used needles and other paraphernalia lying around them. And then there were the times when his mother and Eugene wouldn't come home for days, leaving him with little to no cash for food.

Eugene hardly touched Daemon. This was mostly due to Daemon staying out of the man's way, locked up in his room. But when Eugene did manage to lay a hand on Daemon, it was bad. The scumbag would almost never use his fists. Instead, he'd kick Daemon, use a belt or whatever was around, even clobbering him over the head with a potted house plant.

One night the dirtbag had come home in a real sour mood. Daemon was upstairs and heard the man swearing and breaking things downstairs. A few minutes later, his door was kicked open, splinters of wood from the door frame flying like plastic from the bumper of a wrecked car. Eugene stomped into the room, eyes red, and demanded to know where Daemon had hidden his stash of drugs. Daemon had only fucked with the man's dope once, switching out the weed with oregano so he could sell the stuff to some kids at school—and because it would be funny when the asshole went to smoke it. He figured the man was always so fucked up he wouldn't know the difference. But Eugene had known; his customers too. He beat the shit out of Daemon and threatened that if he ever touched his shit again, he'd kill him.

"I warned you, kid, about fucking with my stash," Eugene said, chest heaving.

Daemon's heart was in his throat, his mouth dry. "I . . . I didn't—"

"You're going to get a beating, but it's up to you how bad it's going to be."

Daemon had been watching porn on his laptop, ready to jerk off, and now he could hardly breathe. Eugene had never kicked his way into his room. The funny thing was that he hadn't touched his drugs.

"I don't know what you're talking about," Daemon said, wanting to sound tough, but his voice cracked, giving away how unnerved he was.

Eugene walked up to his bed, Daemon holding his ground and swallowing hard. "Last chance to make this easier on yourself."

"I swear I didn't take your shit."

Eugene smiled, but his bloodshot eyes remained ice cold. Daemon saw his life flash before his eyes. He knew something really awful was going to happen and braced for impact. Eugene's arm shot forward. The man's fingers clutched a fistful of hair and then Daemon was yanked off his bed. He cried out, his scalp on fire as he was dragged across his room, then out the door and down the hallway to the edge of the stairs. Eugene pulled him to his feet and got in his face.

"I was going to give you another chance back in your room," the man said, his breath a mixture of feces and alcohol that made Daemon's eyes tear. "But you blew it." Daemon was then shoved backward and went sailing down the stairs. His right shoulder hit first, biting agony enveloping it immediately. Then his back came into contact with a stair, and he tumbled ass over head the rest of the way down.

He came to on a stretcher as he was carried to an ambulance that was waiting in his driveway. Apparently, Eugene had come to some sense of mind and called 911, not wanting to go to jail for murder. Daemon's mother had been passed out at the time and only discovered what had happened the following morning when the police paid her a visit and arrested Eugene.

She blamed Daemon for everything and demanded that he tell the police he had tripped on his own and fallen down the stairs and that he lied about Eugene having pushed him.

"I know what really happened, Daemon," she said as he lay bruised with a concussion in his hospital bed. "Eugene told me you threw yourself down the stairs to get back at him. I know you don't like him, but he's good to me and wouldn't lie about something like this."

Daemon couldn't believe what his mother was saying, and when he refused to change his story, she flipped out. She screamed at him and knocked over his food tray and IV stand, ripping the needle out of his arm. Security was called, and she was escorted out of the building. Eugene remained in prison awaiting trial for child endangerment, battery, and attempted murder.

Desperate for drugs and money, Daemon's mother moved to prostituting herself, sometimes even bringing the johns home. One night, two days after his sixteenth birthday, one of the johns started beating his mother.

Daemon had been in his room when he heard his mother come home. He knew by her laugh that she was working, and hearing the man's voice only confirmed it. Normally, he'd go outside and hang out on the front steps smoking cigarette after cigarette, talking on the phone or listening to music, or if it wasn't too late, he'd head over to Bobby's house. But it was late, and he was tired, so he stayed in his room, not only wanting to hear his mother's romp, but needing to, thinking maybe it would do something to him. Make him finally give up on her and leave her to the wolves while he worked on moving away. He'd steal whatever cash he could get his hands on and scram.

After hearing her bedroom door close, the man started yelling, saying how he was going to beat her bloody, while he throat fucked her to unconsciousness. The first smack sounded, and his mother screamed. The floor shook. The sex noises Daemon could deal with, but violence against his mom was another story.

He grabbed his baseball bat—the item stolen from a kid's backyard one night as he made his way home drunk from a keg party—and headed to his mom's room down the hall. He checked the door, found it unlocked, and slowly opened it. Instead of charging in like an angry bull, he wanted to surprise the guy, and snuck up behind him. His mother was on the floor in her bra and panties, crying. Her right eye was already swelling, and her lip was bloody.

Daemon raised the bat to smash the guy on the side of his big head when the floor creaked beneath him. The man spun around, and their eyes met, Daemon having to look up at the behemoth. He swung the bat, but the guy stepped in and took the blow on the upper part of his meaty arm, laughed, and then backhanded him across the room. Daemon slammed into a dresser, knocking a few items off it and losing the bat.

The next thing he knew, the guy was standing over him, a wicked grin on his face and the bat in his hands. "Should've stayed in your room, boy. Do you know what I'm going to do to you in front of your ma? Gonna break your jaw and let it hang. Then your legs so you can't run while you watch me do things to your mom that'll fuck you up for good. Just what my pa did to me. Teach whores a lesson." The man raised the bat, his eyes full of malice. Daemon was about to be introduced to a whole new level of agony when gunfire filled the air.

The man grunted and straightened, his eyebrows coming together in confusion. He coughed and turned around; his footfalls were heavy as if his shoes were made of cement. Another gunshot sounded, and the man's body stiffened. He fell to his knees, and then face-planted to the floor. The bat tumbled away.

When Daemon looked up, he saw his mother holding a revolver, a wisp of gray smoke rising out of the barrel. The gun was Eugene's.

It took some going over, but when all was said and done—Daemon backing up his mom's story of self-defense—she wasn't charged with a crime. He was sent to his uncle's house in Ohio while his mother got the help she needed. His uncle was an alcoholic who slapped his kids and wife around, but never laid a hand on Daemon, even saying how he wished his kids would be more like him. He wound up staying there for a year, moving back home shortly after his seventeenth birthday. His stay in Ohio had done little for his outlook on society.

His cousins had learned to hate him, thanks to their father always comparing him to them. He'd been a loud-mouthed, weed-smoking, truck-driver mouthed asshole—the same person he'd become while living with Eugene—but for some reason his drunk for an uncle practically looked up to him. Maybe it was because he felt bad for him, that his father, his uncle's brother, had left him and then died.

When Daemon returned home, he found that his mother's all-was-right-with-the-world attitude was bullshit. Yeah, she had stopped hooking, but kept doing drugs. And to top it all off, Eugene had moved back in. He'd been living there for a few months. Apparently, the moron had pled down to a lesser charge after making a deal with the feds and informed on his supplier, a bigger fish. He even got to serve his short sentence at a minimum-security prison.

Eugene wasn't the same Eugene Daemon had known. The man had cleaned himself up. He found out he was HIV positive, and Daemon's mother was, too. He helped her kick the habit for the hardcore stuff. Now, the two only smoked of pot.

Daemon didn't know what to make of the situation. He was grateful the man had changed and got his mother straight, but at the same time hoped the guy dropped dead. As far as he was concerned, once an asshole, always an asshole. It was only a matter of time. How they kicked the harder drugs and alcohol but were still able to smoke pot and not have it lead them back to the harder shit he had no idea. But it was working.

On multiple occasions, he thought about killing the man, but ultimately decided to let the HIV lovebirds enjoy their pathetic life together.

He moved out of his room and into the basement, wanting to get as far away from them as possible. It helped a little.

Chapter Three

Bobby went back into the trunk and grabbed another bat. The trio always made sure to have more than one bat when going out for a night of mailbox baseball. It had been during their second night of playing when their bat broke, ending the game early. A valuable lesson had been learned, and they made sure to keep multiple baseball-hitting instruments in the trunk. The idea to use aluminum bats had been shot down by Bobby. Aluminum wouldn't break, and if something was hit hard enough, the shock would travel into the person, possibly resulting in serious injury. The wooden bats would break instead of the bones in a person's body.

Daemon sped up when they hit the playing field, the length of the street where they planned on playing. Bobby donned the helmet and climbed his lanky, six-foot-two frame halfway out the rear window, taking the bat with him. His long, brown hair whipped about wildly. A grin formed across his rat-like face, a combination of delinquent fun and getting to break things. There was a sense of freedom when they played, as if the rules of society didn't apply for the time being, and it felt wonderful. Plus, there was simply something about smashing other people's property that felt good to him. Even when he was younger and stomped on his toys or broke a window by *accident* or pulled apart his mother's dolls, the resulting emotion was one of satisfaction—his frustrations about whatever was bothering him gone.

The first mailbox was coming up. He wedged his left foot under Jade's seat, then kneeled on his own with his right knee and rested his abdomen against the locked door's windowsill. The position allowed for his lower half to be grounded, so he wouldn't fall out while also permitting him to swing with maximum effort.

Bobby howled as his turn in the batter's box was about to begin. He swung hard and fast, leaving his grip loose until the point of impact. The hard plastic material of the black mailbox shattered into numerous shards; the sound musical. The red metal flag that had been attached twanged against the Camry's door and then into the weeds that ran along the road.

Looking back, he saw that a small portion of the mailbox remained. "Fuck!"

Jade poked her head out her window, her purple hair covering her face, and said, "That's a seven, loser."

Before he could tell her to go fuck herself, she was back in the vehicle, so he gave her the finger, knowing she'd see it in the side mirror.

His frustration at not obliterating the mailbox vanished when he realized the next mailbox on the route was Mr. Brewmeyer's, the most hated teacher at Spencer High.

Howard T. Brewmeyer had given Bobby and his friends a very difficult time at school. Hell, the man was an asshole to most students, but seemed to focus on the trio in particular. He handed out detention like candy on Halloween. He constantly degraded students, especially the troublemakers and outcasts. It didn't matter how a person behaved in class. He treated people according to reputation alone, not only how they behaved in school, but how they were perceived around town. The man had often attempted to embarrass Bobby and his friends during class by asking difficult questions—questions not in any textbook, but acting as if the knowledge was common.

Of course, Bobby was bright and knew most of the answers because he read a lot. So Brewmeyer would often turn to Daemon and Jade, the two lovebirds, knowing little to nothing about any subject matter due to their lack of studying. And because Bobby found the material easy, he'd take naps in class, partly to annoy the teacher, but also because he could afford to. The downside was getting woken up by the man when he screamed in his ear or knocked his chair out from under him so that he crashed to the floor. The students would laugh, but Bobby was always okay with it, his main goal accomplished. The man couldn't fail him, so he'd found other ways to screw with Bobby.

And yeah, he'd shot spitballs at the Smart Board, made fart noises when the teacher bent over, and had glued various items—animal bones, bugs, coins, and even a pair of his mom's underwear to Brewmeyer's desk and Smart Board. He'd also gone as far as smearing dog shit across the screen. That had been a bit over the line when it came to fucking with the man, but Bobby had only done it after Brewmeyer fired the first shot by saying he was a spoiled rich kid whose mommy and daddy didn't give a shit about him and never would. Brewmeyer usually fired the first shots when dealing with students, but especially with Bobby, Daemon and Jade. The asshole was simply miserable and thought he was better than everyone. So, all in all, the man deserved all the trouble he received and whatever trouble he was going to get.

Brewmeyer had called Bobby's parents numerous times, hoping to get him in trouble, but they could not have cared less. They never got upset and simply asked him to explain his side of things. Bobby would say that Brewmeyer was jealous because Bobby came from money, or he'd tell them that the man had been in a bad mood that day. His parents nodded and said things like, "That's life among the middle class" or "figures, the man is just jealous, I guess."

Bobby was all but invisible in his house and it took Brewmeyer until the parent-teacher conference to understand this, telling Bobby his parents were scumbags like he and his friends were, only wealthy. Bobby had spit on him and got suspended for two weeks. His parents hadn't even noticed he wasn't in school during that time. If it wasn't for his exorbitant allowance, basically a limitless bank account, he'd hate his parents even more than he already did.

Bobby couldn't believe the anger he still felt toward Brewmeyer. A few years removed from high school and his hatred for the man remained as it always had.

Jade popped her head out the window and yelled, "C'mon, rich boy. Let that fat fuck have it."

"I will if you get out of my way."

Jade stuck her tongue out and wrinkled her nose at him before disappearing back into the car.

The Camry's engine whined harder and the wind blowing over Bobby picked up. He cocked back his arms, holding the bat. Brewmeyer's had been the first mailbox they'd hit, long before they started playing mailbox baseball. They always tossed eggs, rocks or whatever at it as they passed by the man's house, and if curses were harmful, the place would've fallen down years ago.

Bobby adjusted his grip on the handle. His eyes narrowed as his lower row of teeth met his upper. The last two times they had been down this street playing mailbox baseball, it had been Jade's and then Daemon's turn at bat. Waiting for his turn had sucked. Maybe next time they would stop, and all take turns beating the crap out of the thing. But for now, the glory was all his.

The mailbox was large, rectangular and bright orange. Plain in design. Ugly. This was strange. Brewmeyer had always had beautiful mailboxes, from replicas of battleships to Mississippi riverboats to classic cars. Bobby couldn't blame the man for changing to something ordinary, though, for who would want to keep spending a lot of money on something, only to see it destroyed. The asshole had wised-up. Bought an inexpensive one.

Shit, Bobby felt a bit let down. A bit of disappointment. Now he was more pissed at the guy for robbing him of his pleasure. Muscles tensed; bat gripped tightly. He swung the wood as hard as he could. Even though it was cheap, he was still going to get satisfaction out of destroying the man's property.

The bat collided with the side of the bright orange box, only to come to a sudden stop. A reverberating shock traveled into Bobby's hands and up his arms and into his head. He cried out in pain as the bat shattered. A large, jagged chunk shot back into his face, whacking the hockey mask with hammer-like force. Splinters of wood filled the air, a few toothpick-sized slivers making it through the hockey mask's holes and into his skin.

He fell forward and nearly out of the window but was able to grab onto the top of the door and hold on. Arm and back muscles straining, he pulled himself back into the car.

The Camry skidded to a stop.

"What the hell happened?" Jade asked.

"I have no idea," Bobby said. "The mailbox was like a solid block of steel." He pulled off the mask and sat back, breathing heavily. He stretched his arms and made fists; his fingers stiff. "The bat exploded. My arms are killing me. If I didn't have the mask on, I'd be out cold on the side of the road."

Jade turned on the dome light. "Dude, you're white as a ghost."

Daemon turned around and looked at Bobby. He reached back and grabbed the hockey mask, seeing a scuff mark where the chunk of wood had connected.

"Thing saved my life, man," Bobby said.

Daemon put the car in reverse and backed it up to where the mailbox still stood. "That ain't no mailbox," he said. "And look at the pole; it's got to be at least six inches thick. What mailbox needs that?" He looked past the orange box at the house. There were no lights on. Something odd was definitely going on.

Daemon opened the driver's side door and stepped out.

"Where are you going?" Jade asked.

Not answering her, he walked around the vehicle to the mailbox. There wasn't a mark on it. He wrapped his knuckles on the door and felt its sturdiness, the thing solid steel. Bending low, he felt that the pole the box rested on was steel too, the two items welded together.

Standing, he heard the slightest hint of laughter. The sound was coming from the house. Then: "Gotcha, you little piss-ants."

The voice was low, but Daemon recognized it. Not that anyone else lived in Brewmeyer's place. The asshole had set them up. He was a Waiter, but not a Chaser.

"That's the last mailbox of mine you'll destroy," the voice said, coming somewhere from in the darkened house.

Daemon peered into the blackness, the moonlight making its way through the trees in the yard. He saw no one. The man didn't have the stones to come outside. He was in the house, watching through one of the windows. Why would he taunt his attackers? Had he called the police and was stalling, hoping Daemon would stick around for a confrontation that would never happen?

Shit—what if the guy was recording him? Had recorded the whole event? It wouldn't matter if Daemon took off before the cops arrived. Then again, there was no property damage. If anything, Bobby might be able to sue the asshole for bodily injury. Of course, he'd have to get the attention of his parents. Yeah, right.

A searing heat filled Daemon's gut. He was pissed, a furnace ready to blow. Brewmeyer's laughing continued, fueling Daemon's anger. He wanted to threaten the man, tell him his house was next to be continuously hit. But he held his tongue, turned around and got back in the car, then drove away.

Chapter Four

After dropping off Bobby—his arms still aching—Daemon drove to Jade's house, where they fucked like angry rabbits. The sex was fierce, the kind without foreplay. Daemon yanked down Jade's jean shorts and underwear in one motion before taking her from behind. He rammed into her, thrusting while pulling her to him in rhythmic fashion. Jade was still wet from the night's events. Violence always got her hot. She loved it when he pulled her hair, so he did.

When she begged for him to smack her ass, he obliged and when it wasn't hard enough; he increased the force of his blows. Banging and pulling and smacking, all the actions making Jade scream with pleasure. Her cheeks were still a bit sore from two nights ago when she had Daemon bite them while they sucked each other off. He'd broken skin at one point, and Jade came hard, causing him to explode. Her screams of pleasure became gurgles of ecstasy as he filled her mouth.

When they were finished screwing, his seed filling her where she couldn't get pregnant, they flopped to the bed, slick with sweat. Lying there, they shared a joint. It was something they usually did after an intense session to further relax. But neither the sex nor the pot did much to calm down Daemon.

Unable to let go, he sat up quickly. No matter how hard he tried, he couldn't stop thinking of Brewmeyer and how the man had won. It was only a battle, but it was high school all over again. The man trying to up himself against his students. Prove he was better and make them feel like shit.

Jade hugged Daemon from behind, laying her head against his back. She rubbed his right pectoral muscle. "You're so tense, babe." She nibbled his ear, but he shrugged her off. "Hey," she yelled and swatted him.

"Fuck off."

"What the hell is the matter with you?"

"Brewmeyer. I haven't been able to calm down since the incident. Can't get that fuckhead out of my mind. I mean, he thinks he's so smart. That he won."

"Fuck him," Jade said. "He's a loser. Lives alone. We'll get him again. Fuck up his car or something."

Daemon wanted nothing more than to get dressed, head over to Brewmeyer's place and. .. What? What would he do? Smash the guy's car? Break windows? Break in and destroy the inside? None of those things would be wise. At least not now.

One of the reasons they hadn't gotten caught for the mailboxes was because they had been smart regarding how they went about it. They stuck to Bobby's plan about not returning to the same street for at least a month, though for certain ones, they usually only waited three weeks.

Another problem could arise if Brewmeyer had recorded them. Even if there was no property damage, the cops still might come after them—if only to harass them. Even charge them with the other smashed mailboxes. But if the asshole had been able to make Daemon out when he got out of his car, or had indeed recorded them, the cops would've been at their door already. Brewmeyer wouldn't wait. Daemon had been careless getting out of the car and couldn't do such things in the future, not without a mask on.

He shot to his feet as Jade's arm began to slink around his neck and paced the room.

"C'mon, babe," Jade said, shaking her tits. "Come back to bed. You just need to come again. I'll do all the work, blow you and swallow. I know how much you like that."

He stopped pacing and faced her, cheek muscles bulging. "Don't you get it? No amount of sex is going to help me. I need to hurt that fat fuck."

Nipples erect, Jade climbed off the bed and walked over to him. Laying a hand on his chest, she said, "We will get him. Don't you think I want that too? After what he did to us, to Bobby? There's nothing we can do about it now. So let me take care of you."

She leaned in and kissed him on his lips.

He offered nothing in return, but remained where he was.

Grinning, her dark brown eyes sparkling wickedly, she planted a kiss on his chin, then his throat before she made her way down his defined abs and finally to his semi-hard penis with her scent still on it. Using her tongue, she flicked the tip and tasted herself. An electric-like spark of excitement exploded through her, causing her pussy to moisten and nipples to further harden.

When she continued to tease him, he grabbed her by her hair and shoved her face into his crotch. She gulped down his cock and worked it with his help. She loved the rough treatment, the feeling of being forced to blow him, even though she wanted to. Using her fingers, she played with herself. Before long, she felt his soft flesh swell and knew he was about to explode, and when he did, her mouth filled with his salty fluids as she came too.

Swallowing, she wiped the dribble from her bottom lip and stood. He kissed her hard, their tongues mingling. He tasted himself and then they separated.

"Feel a little better?" she asked.

"Yeah, a little."

"C'mon," she said, took him by the hand and guided him to the bed. There, they lay and shared a cigarette.

"Did I ever tell you that you're the best?" Daemon asked.

Jade finished tugging on her smoke and said, "Yeah, after every fucking blow job."

He laughed. "Well, it's true." She passed the cigarette to him. He accepted it and took a drag before snuffing it out in the small glass ashtray on the nightstand. Jade moved, resting her head on his chest, and was asleep in minutes. Daemon lay there, trying not to think about Brewmeyer. He reached over, shut off the light, and concentrated on Jade's gentle snoring, hoping it would set his mind enough at ease so he could fall asleep. Just as he was about to reach la-la land, his cell phone rang. He'd forgotten to shut off the ringer.

Without lifting her head up, Jade said, "Whoever that is dies."

Daemon was pissed Jade had been woken. He reached over to see who was calling, ready to tell whoever it was to fuck off and die when he saw it was Bobby.

Putting the phone to his ear, he said," Jade's going to kill you, man. This better be good."

"They're dead, man," Bobby said.

"Who's dead?"

"The dudes driving the SUV that chased us."

"Who's dead?" Jade asked, not moving.

Daemon ignored her, concentrating on what Bobby was saying.

"I heard cops talking over the police scanner," Bobby said. "The driver and passenger died at the scene."

Daemon remained silent, unsure of what to say. People died all the time. People he didn't know. The people driving the SUV were no different from someone halfway around the globe dying, except that they lived in the same area as him. The other difference was that the SUV people had been Waiters and stupid. In today's world, who would be dumb enough to chase after someone who just destroyed their mailbox? People were crazy. Hadn't the SUV people realized that? And besides, he despised Waiters. Fuck them. He was glad they were dead. Truly glad.

"Did you hear me, dude?" Bobby asked.

"Yeah, I heard you. They're dead. Good riddance. Two less morons in the world."

Jade lifted her head off his chest and looked at him. "Who the fuck died?"

"But we caused it," Bobby said.

"Shut the fuck up," Daemon said, sitting up and throwing Jade off him.

"What the fuck?" she shouted and shoved him.

"This ain't a conversation to have on the phone," Daemon said. "I thought you were supposed to be the smart one?"

"No one's listening to our call, Daemon," Bobby said. "We aren't on some watch list."

"Whatever," Daemon said, grabbing his pack of smokes off the night-stand. "Just drop it. There was an accident. People died. Oh well. If you hear anything about the *individuals* involved, then call me back. Otherwise, I need to get some sleep." Daemon ended the call and returned his phone to the charger on the nightstand.

With slits for eyes and lips but a thin line, Jade was sitting up and staring at him. Her tattooed arms were crossed over her chest. Daemon focused on her forearm where the inked version of Jade as a baby resting in a bassinet coffin lay. A serpent tongue protruded from the mouth. After getting it, she'd told him that until her death, the snake would remain inside her and cause her to do and love evil. He didn't know about all that, but he loved it and her.

Knowing she was pissed at how he treated her, he said, "The Waiters who chased us are dead."

Jade's eyes widened as her lips parted. "You mean, from the crash?"

"Apparently."

"Damn." Her eyes moved around the room, focusing on this and that. Daemon could tell she was processing what she'd heard. He was beginning to feel a bit worried and asked if she was all right.

"I don't know what I am," she said. "I wasn't expecting to be woken up by such news. It's . . . weird." She said 'weird' as if she were stoned out of her mind.

"Yeah, I guess. But fuck it. Dead's dead. Nothing we can do about it."

"Yeah, but we caused it. We're responsible."

"They started it," Daemon said, lighting a cigarette. Inhaling, he tossed the lighter on the nightstand, where it slid to a stop against the clock radio. "The world is full of psychos and shit." As he spoke, smoke exited his mouth in uneven waves. "They performed an act of vigilantism. That's illegal. We defended ourselves." He paused, taking another drag, waiting for Jade to say something. When she didn't speak and continued to stare into space, he asked her if she cared that they were dead.

"No. I don't, actually. Can you believe it?"

Daemon felt relief flood through him. As he continued to stare at her, her cheeks rippled as a smile formed on her pretty face. She looked sinister, like a salivating feline ready to pounce on an unsuspecting mouse.

She giggled. "I. .. I think I just came."

"You what?"

"I just had an orgasm. Thinking about what we caused. I fucking love it." Her eyes were bright. "We killed people. Took lives, and we didn't even mean to. Imagine if we had meant to."

Daemon nodded; an eyebrow cocked.

"I'm so fucking horny right now," Jade said, her chest rising and falling with haste.

"It is hot, isn't it?"

"Fuck yeah it is." Jade snatched the almost-finished cigarette from his lips and stuck the butt between hers. Inhaling, she then said, "Maybe next time we can be more direct about fucking shit up," and then snuffed out the cancer stick on her tongue, tossing the butt onto the floor.

The two lovers stared at each other, Jade's crotch soaked, Daemon's cock rock hard. She shoved him to the bed, climbed on top of him and slid his throbbing member into her, riding wildly until they both came.

CHAPTER FIVE

THE NEXT DAY, DAEMON and Jade hopped into the Camry and headed over to Bobby's house. The wealthy kid's parents had been away for a week and weren't going to be home again for another month. The affluent couple had gone on a business/vacation tour of Europe—of course, not asking Bobby if he'd like to tag along. Instead, they had left a typed letter about their plans on the fridge. A number of credit cards and stacks of cash were on the counter. Bobby had his own bank account with plenty of greenbacks in it, but his parents seemed to love throwing money at him in other ways, as if the physical sight of plastic and cash showed how much love they had for him.

Daemon drove along the quarter-mile long driveway through dense woods, the pavement twisting and turning like the body of a gigantic snake. It opened up to ten acres of sprawling lawn that surrounded the five-bedroom, four-bathroom, three-fireplace and five-car garage mansion.

The structure was of modern design, boxy, and had large, wall-encompassing windows that allowed for views of much of the first level. Bobby hated that anyone walking by could see inside, causing him to always keep the blinds closed despite the house being surrounded by acres of woods and not visible from the road.

After parking the car, they went around back.

Bobby was lying on a sunbathing chair poolside, his flesh the color of chalk. His right wrist was wrapped in a bandage.

"Mommy fix you up?" Jade asked, laughing as she took a seat on one of the chairs positioned around a glass table.

"Fuck you," Bobby said. "My parents aren't even home."

"I know. I was joking." Jade plucked a few grapes from a bowl of fruit that was sitting at center table, then leaned back and threw her legs up onto the glass top.

"Still hurts?" Daemon asked as he pulled out the chair closest to his long-time friend.

Bobby held out his injured hand. "Yeah, but it ain't broken. So, physically, I'm good."

"Fucking Brewmeyer," Daemon said. "We need to get that piece of shit."

"I'd love to make him eat my shit," Bobby said, his tone hollow. He ran a hand over his head, smoothing back his long hair. "Literally, shove my shit down his ugly face and then break his ribs."

"Sounds like a plan," Jade said. "But I ain't getting near your shit."

Daemon withdrew a lighter from his jeans pocket and extended it toward Jade, who had placed a cigarette between her lips. Using his thumb, he rolled the flint and produced a flame.

"What a fucking gentleman," she said, her cigarette bouncing up and down as she spoke. She leaned forward and let the flame do its thing.

Daemon popped one of his own cigarettes into his mouth and lit it. He pinched the butt between his teeth, ready to chew the thing, but took a long, hard drag instead. The coals at the end burned bright and fast.

Bobby was his best friend. They had always been there for each other. His friend had been attacked. And not just by any *someone*, but a despised someone. Something had to be done about it.

They had met in the sixth grade during detention. Bobby had only been in town a couple weeks. That day he'd been wearing a Slayer T-shirt, and they discovered they liked the same music—heavy metal—as well as the same girl, Delilah Sparks. She was completely out of their league, but it didn't stop them from telling each other all the sexual things they wanted to do to her.

Daemon had had no idea how wealthy Bobby was until a month after they started hanging out. They never went to the guy's house, and it wasn't until Daemon finally did go, that Bobby had told him that his parents were fucked up and could be really judgmental assholes. Then again, they could be just fine. Bobby never knew which version of his parents would show up when he brought friends home.

Daemon had come to learn that Bobby, as a tall skinny kid with pasty skin and long hair, didn't have many friends in his previous school. It was mostly a preppy jock school, a place where Bobby stood out like a zit on a prom queen. Spencer High School had its jocks, geeks and other groups, but it also had its metal heads and troublemakers. Bobby had finally found a true friend and a place where he belonged. In turn, Daemon had found someone he could trust and treat like a brother.

They got high on Bobby's home grown weed, occasionally sprinkling it with angel dust, before moving on to LSD and cocaine. Bobby could get whatever they wanted; his money stream endless. Normally, Daemon would've taken advantage and drained as much money as possible from the kid, keeping him as a friend only for that very reason. But with Bobby, he felt like he'd be ripping off a member of his family. Daemon rejected the kid's money until Bobby wouldn't shut up about what a pleasure it was to spend his parents' seemingly endless supply of cash.

When Daemon finally met Bobby's parents and they barely gave him a glance, he realized they were no better than his own parents. Instead of all the physical and verbal abuse, Bobby received silence. The guy was left hollow, with the pain of emptiness. Bobby was the invisible boy, a ghost, lucky enough to at least have money. Daemon would've traded places with him in a second, even though he knew the implication about grasses always being greener. The two became inseparable, closer than any blood brothers could be.

It wasn't long before the town knew that the Weatherly family had money. Kids started using Bobby. He had more fake friends than Barbie. Having seen enough, Daemon lost his cool one day after Gerald Higgins borrowed a hundred bucks and refused to pay it back. When the moron went around school showing off his newly acquired sneakers, Daemon decided to make an example out of the kid. Not only did he beat the shit out of Higgins, but he stole his sneakers, filled them with dog shit later that night, then forced the kid to put them on the next day and walk along the hallway singing how he was full of shit. Daemon was suspended, but it had been worth it. After that, people treated Bobby with a lot more respect.

As the boys got older and trouble grew more serious, Bobby's money came in handy when Daemon started getting arrested. The crimes weren't serious—public intoxication, destruction of property, public urination, spray painting—until the night he got in a fight with a redneck who knew his mom back when she was hooking. The scumbag said how much he missed fucking her in her ass, then watching her blow him dry. Daemon threw the first punch, but the guy was much bigger and didn't go down. They exchanged blows until

Daemon pulled out a knife and stabbed the guy in the stomach. In the end, Daemon received probation.

Eventually, Daemon got a job at a garage outside of town where he put his mechanic skills to use. As much as he hated working and loved sitting around getting high and letting his mind melt away, he knew having a job where he could do something he enjoyed would be a good thing. He'd always loved working on cars and understood that he'd never amount to being some kind of executive or lawyer or doctor. But regardless of Daemon getting a paycheck, and despite his wanting to pay his own way, Bobby paid for everything.

"Fuck it, Daemon," Bobby had said. "I love putting my asshole parents' money to good and bad use. Or have you forgotten?" They both laughed at that, knowing that most of the money was spent on partying.

Daemon's thoughts came back to the present. His eyes focused on the bandage that covered Bobby's wrist, then on Bobby's face where a number of cuts took up residence. He shook his head, seething with rage. He needed to scream. Someone had come after his brother and almost seriously hurt him. Shit, Bobby could've been killed. What if he'd fallen out of the car? Or hadn't had a hockey mask on when the chunk of bat flew into his face? Or if a jagged piece of the bat had sliced his jugular?

A stinging heat sparked in Daemon's palms. Looking down at his hands, he saw his nails had dug into his flesh.

"Babe, are you okay?" Jade asked. "You look like you need to kill someone."

He nodded. "Yeah, I think I do."

"Speaking of killing," Bobby said, sitting up and putting his bare feet on the cement. "Are we all okay with what happened last night?"

"It made me wet," Jade said.

"We killed people," Bobby said. "It's not something to take lightly."

"Are you sure you're okay with what we did?" Daemon asked. "Because the dead are dead. There ain't nothing we can do for them. And those motherfuckers were assholes looking for trouble. They got what was coming to them."

Bobby nodded. "I was a little freaked out last night. I couldn't sleep. Kept listening to the scanner. But it wasn't because those people were dead. I realized I was all fucked up because I didn't want to get caught. Prison just isn't for me, you know?"

Daemon focused on his friend, looking for a sign that the man was bullshitting. Trying to fit in with him and Jade. He loved Bobby and would do anything for the guy, but he needed to make sure the dude was truly okay with what happened because the plans he had were going to lead them down a fun-filled, crazy path of notoriety; something they could not come back from.

"We all had a hand in those fuckers' deaths," Jade said, clearly wanting part of the credit for the act.

Daemon pulled out the pipe he'd brought with him from one of his jean pockets.

"Time to smoke up," he said. Jade eagerly agreed. Bobby tossed him a bag of weed. Daemon packed the bowl before bringing it to his lips. He flicked the lighter, sparking it to life, and inhaled as the green plant glowed orange and burned. After filling his lungs, he held in the smoke for a few seconds, then exhaled and said, "We're all killers, at least to some degree. Indirectly or directly. Who gives a shit? Doesn't matter. The cops ain't after us. We left no trace. The only thing that could be bad for us, as far as the cops are concerned, is Brewmeyer."

"Fuck him," Jade said, taking the pipe from Daemon.

"His place is nowhere near where the accident happened," Bobby said. "Unless he saw you when you got out of the car and told the cops. If he did, then the law will assume we're the ones who've been smashing mailboxes. The cops will at least haul us in for questioning."

Daemon shook his head. "Fuck. I was thinking there was a chance the fat fuck Brewmeyer had been recording when we smashed his steel box, including recording me when I got out. He'd want something to watch over and over again to get his kicks on how smart he is. And if he knows it was us, he might leak it to the cops for all we know."

"We'd get nailed for the mailboxes and possibly the accident," Bobby said.

"That sneaky piece of shit," Jade said, blowing out smoke.

"We don't know if he recorded us, let alone saw our identities," Bobby said. "Though it was dark and his yard tree-filled, the moon was full and the sky clear. We don't know what the camera was able to pick up. Remember, the man loves getting others in trouble, punishing students and people he dislikes. So why hasn't he called the cops yet?"

"He doesn't want to get in trouble for his own mailbox stunt," Daemon said, taking the bowl from Jade.

"Right," Jade said. "Like that burglar who broke into that family's home and got hurt and then sued and got like a lot of money."

"That was bullshit," Bobby said. "An old urban legend. If I'd have gotten injured, I'd be shit out of luck as far as suing."

"No, it was real," Jade insisted. "Don't be naïve."

"Whatever," Daemon said, exhaling smoke as he talked. "What we need is to be sure he ain't got nothing on us."

"So what? Break into his house and look for a fucking video camera?" Bobby asked.

"Exactly," Daemon said, tapping out the ash from the bowl.

"And we should break Brewmeyer's arms and legs while we're at it," Jade said, sitting up, her eyes beaming like a proud parent's.

"That's why I love the shit out of you, babe," Daemon said. "You're always ready to shine."

"If you guys are serious, then we're going to have to be smart about it," Bobby said. "Plan it out. Wait and watch. Be patient—"

"Screw that," Jade said, and threw the grape she was rolling back and forth on the table at Bobby, hitting him in the forehead. "I say we storm in like Vikings. Rape and plunder."

Daemon stared at her.

"What?" she asked, shrugging.

"You're a sick bitch, you know that?"

"Yes, you tell me that all the time and I love hearing it." Jade smiled and batted her lashes.

Bobby groaned; his patience obviously thin. "We can't bust in there. It needs to be calculated and clean."

"Don't worry, man," Daemon said. "It will be carefully planned out. We don't want to get caught. I've been itching to get revenge on Brewmeyer forever. I'm talking real revenge. Something that will make mailbox baseball look like the game it is. We'll teach that asshole a lesson and make sure we walk away clean. Nothing will lead the cops to us."

"So, we're really doing this?" Bobby asked.

"Hell yeah, we are," Jade said, pumping her fist.

Chapter Six

After Daemon spoke about what he intended to do, Bobby came up with a plan. The first part involved waiting at least a month before any action was taken. The plan was nothing incredibly sophisticated, but it was thorough.. Although it was still unknown who the mailbox baseball vagrants were, the authorities surmised that the traffic accident involving the SUV and two deaths was the result of the lesser crime resulting in the larger one.

Buckshot was found in the truck's front end and blown-out tires. The surviving wife of the driver told police that her husband and his brother-in-law were waiting to catch the people who had been smashing their mailboxes, wound up chasing them and getting killed. This moved the investigation way up on the police's radar. Still, no one came knocking on any of the trio's doors.

Knowing they would need more supplies, Bobby purchased a re-loadable Visa card. A number of items were purchased from various online stores. Everything was shipped to Jade's uncle's house, the place Jade resided when she wasn't at Daemon's. Her uncle was a full-time drunk, specializing in never leaving his house, never wearing a shirt and somehow surviving off his social security disability payments on account of his being in a car accident that took the use of his legs. The items ordered wouldn't be touched by the man and left on the front porch for Jade when she came home.

Among the supplies obtained: multiple pairs of black leather gloves, a few cases of various colored Plasti Dip canisters—their assortment of colors running low, and ski masks. Daemon was going to use it to disguise whichever vehicle was used when they went out for a night of mischief. Add in the license plate change and they would be golden. When they were done for the evening, the coating of Plasti-Dip would be peeled off, leaving the original paint job intact and unblemished.

Chapter Seven

Dressed in black garb and carrying backpacks with their supplies, the trio of friends climbed into the newly painted maroon Camry and drove toward Brewmeyer's house. They parked a few acres away from the teacher's property on an old, weed-strewn dirt road that no one used anymore and where the car was completely hidden from the road.

From there, they donned black leather gloves, and using the red-lensed military flashlights Bobby had purchased, they made their way through the woods toward the teacher's property. Bobby let loose an occasional grunt whenever Jade, who was ahead of him, let a branch whack him in the face or some other part of his body.

"Cut it out, asshole," he said.

"Go around me. I can't worry about your pussy-ass. By the way, Bobby, these flashlights are fucking cool as fuck."

"The red lenses allow us enough light to see by while keeping anyone from seeing us from afar."

"Really?" Jade said, sounding overly sarcastic. "You think because I'm a chick I don't know shit about army shit?"

Bobby shook his head, moved past Jade, and walked next to Daemon, who said, "She's a real bitch tonight, eh?"

"No comment," Bobby said, focused on the task ahead.

"Thanks, sweetie," Jade said and swatted Daemon on his ass.

The houses along Merdock Road were practically made to be robbed. Each abode had at least a few acres of thickly wooded land between them, and behind the long row of houses was nothing but swampland.

Daemon felt his pulse quicken with every step. The three weeks he'd had to wait only fueled his need for vengeance, and he was ready to burst with the rage and hate he felt for the teacher. It was difficult not to charge ahead, Brewmeyer's place like a magnet and he a chunk of devilish metal.

When they reached the backyard, the despised teacher's two-story house came into view. From the tree line, they scanned the structure for security cameras.

"I don't see any," Daemon said.

"Yeah, place looks clear, though we should check the front for cameras too," Bobby said. "We really should've done all this a few days earlier."

"Stop your worrying," Jade said.

As they made their way along the property line, Daemon noticed the empty driveway and stopped. "Shit."

"What?" Jade asked.

"He's not home," Bobby answered, clearly noticing too. "We should've done a drive and made sure his car was here."

"Boo hoo," Jade said, and stomped the ground like a spoiled child. "All this way and no one to torture."

"At least we know he didn't go to the cops, and we can guess, more than likely, that he didn't record us," Bobby said.

"Unless he was using a handheld camera," Daemon said. "It's why we should go inside and make sure."

"Damn it," Bobby said. "This isn't going down according to plan. He was supposed to be home—we knock at his door, he opens it, and we bum rush him. No alarm is sounded. If we break in now and an alarm goes off . . ."

"So, we'll figure out if he's got one," Jade said. "Toss a rock at a window. Duh. If a siren goes off, we'll leave."

"Me and Jade will go in through the rear," Daemon said.

"I love it when you go in my rear, babe," Jade said, grinning.

Daemon grinned at her, then continued. "If there's an alarm, we'll come right back. In the meantime, you stay here and keep a lookout. If the dickface comes home, call me. We'll hurry out the back before he knows it."

"It's risky," Bobby said, rubbing his chin.

"Sometimes, man, you just got to go with what's provided." Daemon motioned towards the house. "I mean, the asshole ain't home. We got nothing to worry about with a lookout."

"If I'm involved, I want to have fun too," Bobby said.

"After we fuck up a room or two, I'll send Jade out to switch with you. Sound good?"

"Just leave me his bedroom," Bobby said. "I want to take a huge dump on his pillow."

"Incredible," Jade said.

"What is?" Bobby asked.

"That you can shit on demand like that. Must be so useful."

"It is."

"You'll have to teach me that trick someday."

"All right," Daemon said. "Time to do this." He slid off his backpack and let it fall to the grass. Unzipping the bag, he pulled out the hockey mask and handed it to Jade, then handed Bobby his surgical cap and mask before pulling the tan-colored stocking he'd purchased over his head. Immediately, he felt a surge of adrenaline, as if the stocking held some kind of ancient power. Looking at the others, he couldn't help but grin at how wicked they all looked, and together they would make one hell of a frightening bunch of . . . What? What were they, exactly? Vandals? Punks? Soon-to-be killers? He certainly had more than destruction on his mind. Jade too. But Bobby? It didn't matter because they were an evolving evil that would grow like a tumor and wreak havoc upon all in their path. This was only the beginning.

From their place by the tree line, Daemon and Jade headed to the house and checked for security devices and signs that stated the house was protected by so-and-so company. Finding nothing of the sort, Daemon rang the front doorbell while Jade crouched a few feet off to the right behind a row of neatly trimmed lilac bushes. When no one came to the door, he knocked and rang the doorbell again, making sure no one was home. If a light had come on from inside the house and the door opened, he would have bum rushed Brewmeyer.

Assured the place was vacant—they could make noise and take their time—they went around to the backyard and tried kicking in the backdoor. After a few good whacks without it opening, Daemon retrieved a hammer from his backpack.

"Care to do the honors?" he asked, holding the tool out.

"Yes, please," Jade said, her voice slightly distorted through the hockey mask. She took the hammer, walked up to the window on the right side of the house, and swung. The glass shattered, the still atmosphere along with it. "Such a lovely sound." She giggled and then knocked out the jagged pieces that were sticking out of the windowpane.

As soon as the window was cleared, the duo climbed inside.

They took a few moments to allow their eyes to adjust to the darker surroundings and saw that they were in a living room, standing behind a sofa. Bookshelves lined the wall to their left. Straight ahead was a flat screen—the television a measly thirty-two inches in size. Daemon thought it was way too small for such a large room and it made him hate Brewmeyer even more. Why wouldn't the asshole want to experience home theater-like quality?

Past the television was a nook where an ornate-looking desk took up space. A laptop rested on top; its lid open but the screen was dark.

Jade climbed over the sofa. "Looks like a great place to start," she said and hurled the hammer at the television. The screen cracked, resulting in numerous lightning bolt-like fractures spreading across it, but the glass remained in place. Jade hurried over, picked up the hammer and began smashing the television and giggling madly.

Daemon pulled out his hunting knife and plunged it into the sofa. He dragged the blade across the seat cushions, then slashed the back ones, shredding the fabric with ease. When he was satisfied with his work, the piece of furniture looking as if it had been in a fight with a tiger, he found Jade jumping up and down on the smashed and broken flat screen that she'd ripped off the wall. Glass and plastic littered the carpet around her.

Daemon moved to the bookcases, found that they weren't bolted to the wall, and pulled one forward. Books spilled out as its own momentum sent it crashing to the floor. After the second went down, he turned his attention to the unmarked white walls. Using his knife, he stabbed and slashed them. Realizing his fists and feet would do more damage, he punched and kicked, creating large, jagged holes. Tearing into the walls and seeing his fists and boots covered in white sheetrock dust was somewhat euphoric, as if the house's blood was on his hands, and he imagined to a degree that this must be how a killer feels when the blood of a victim is set free.

Jade joined in, sending the claw-end of her hammer into the defenseless walls and ripping them apart. Hanging pictures were obliterated. Glass flew about like confetti. An expensive-looking painting of an elderly lady sitting in a rocking chair holding a yellow cat of all things was made worthless.

From the living room—if that's what it was—they made their way along a hall, knocking down more paintings and gouging the walls with hammer and fists. They passed a laundry room and the back door and then walked into the kitchen. A small white kitchen table and matching chairs sat across from them. The tabletop was decorated with circular woven placemats and a salt and pepper shaker, each in the shape of a naked woman. The asses jutted out and there was a clear plug where the butthole would normally be. Each shaker had tremendously large breasts with half-inch long nipples. The right shaker had a hole at the end of each nipple. The left shaker had three holes around each nipple. Jade picked one up.

"Fucking guy's a total perv," she said, then pocketed both pieces. "I know we're not supposed to take anything, but c'mon, these are too cool."

"I won't tell if you won't," Daemon said. He lifted the stocking, so his mouth was free, then lifted Jade's hockey mask and kissed her. When they separated, Jade said he looked so fucking creepy and wanted him to wear it the next time they fucked. Daemon grabbed her ass, pulled her close and barked. "I want you now."

"First, we got a house to destroy."

Lowering their masks back in place, they looked around.

A microwave, toaster and coffeemaker sat on the counter next to the sink, the counter ending where the stove began. Above the counter and stove were wooden cabinets. Across from the stove was a towering refrigerator. The air smelled like lemons and oozed cleanliness. Not a dish was in the sink, nor a crumb on the counter or table.

"Fucking guy's a neat freak," Jade said, sounding annoyed when the two separated from each other.

"Good, it'll make the asshole that much more upset when he finds his place all fucked up."

Jade opened a cabinet door and snatched a ceramic plate. She held it up and then let it drop to the floor, where it exploded into multiple shards. "Oops."

Daemon looked around for where he should begin as Jade continued to smash dinnerware and giggle. With the fridge practically calling to him, he opened the door and eyed the milk. Grabbing the container, he poured the cow-produced contents over the room, splashing the table, chairs, floor, and walls. Next, he grabbed a pan of lasagna, and using a large spoon he found in one of the drawers, began flinging the Italian food all over the place. Finished with that, he flung the pan into one of the walls. It clanged loudly, made a divot, and then hit the floor.

Turning back to the fridge, he thought removing one item at a time would take too long. He needed to cause as much damage as possible and as quickly as possible while still enjoying himself. Brewmeyer could come home at any moment.

He remembered seeing a meat-tenderizer in the drawer where he found the spoon and retrieved the meat-pounding tool.

Returning to the fridge, he swung open the door and began smashing everything inside. Orange juice exploded from cartons. Cans of soda spewed their contents. A bag of salad was tossed while a container of baked beans was smashed. The glass shelves shattered. Despite the danger of getting cut, Daemon went wild. The leather on his hands would protect him as long as he was somewhat careful, the gloves holding up nicely so far, despite his punching holes in the walls. However, being amped up and seeing all the wonderful destruction, he was unable to help himself and went a little crazier, smashing and swinging and yelling. Vegetables and all sorts of items were splattered about, covering him and the floor at his feet. But he didn't care because it was so much damn fun.

When he was finished, having not taken more than a minute or so, the fridge was a hollow shell, all the broken items at the bottom and pouring out onto the floor. As he took a moment to admire his work, he heard the sound of glass shatter from down the exiting hallway. Turning around, he saw that Jade was gone.

Holding onto the tenderizer, he hurried down the hall and saw Jade toss a book out a broken window—the window facing the front of the house.

"What the hell are you doing?" he said.

Jade spun around and started laughing. "You look ridiculous, like some kid at camp who got into a food fight."

Daemon shook himself off and wiped his stocking and chest. "Don't throw shit outside. We don't need anyone seeing books or whatever on the lawn."

"Who's going to see anything from the road? It's dark out?"

"We don't need Brewmeyer to see anything on his lawn when he comes home. We want it to be a surprise, remember?"

"Oh, yeah." Jade went over to the window. "Well, you don't have to worry about him seeing anything on the lawn because the book is on the driveway."

"Wonderful."

Jade started knocking out the rest of the window's glass.

"Cut it out, Jade."

"I'm only cleaning the window of glass, so he won't see it's broken. It'll only look open or super clean if his car's headlights shine on the house. His being such a neat freak, he might notice a broken window, right?"

"Good thinking, sweetie."

As Jade stepped back from the window, headlights lit up the room and the sound of an engine grew louder.

"Shit, you jinxed us," Daemon said. "The motherfucker must be home."

"Damn it," Jade said. "I wasn't even close to finished with this place."

Daemon's phone rang. Checking it, he saw that Bobby was calling. "Yeah, dude, what's up?"

"He's home. Get the hell out of there."

Daemon glanced at Jade. His blood was pumping, heart pounding against his breastbone and it felt delicious. "Nah., I think we're going to stay."

Chapter Eight

Howard Brewmeyer was having a wonderful evening. Hell, he'd had a great day, too. Failed a third of his students, dealt a bunch detentions, and got to spend last period staring at Kendra Souter's nipples as they tented her tight, practically see-through, pink top. He'd taken a few pictures, zooming in really close, using his cell phone while the group was told to read an article he'd handed out. It was bullshit, a spur-of-the-moment thing, so he could snap pictures of Kendra's tits without being seen.

He'd gotten a few of her face too, and would video edit them all onto one of the porn stars from one of his videos, allowing him the pleasure of masturbating to his hot student's naked body. He'd had to resort to this newer tactic—having already built up quite the library of porn-altered videos—ever since the camera he'd installed in the girl's locker room had been found. The principal and his crack committee believed it was set by a student, and to avoid a scandal, they kept the incident among themselves.

Whacking off to semi-imaginative naked Kendra and shooting his load onto her face as she moaned his name was something he looked forward to that evening after a few beers. But then, when he went down to Dwight's Bar and Grill—a real redneck shithole with a vomit-stained pool table and rat-infested basement—he wound up getting lucky. Lucky that a twenty-two-year-old hottie—if not a smidge on the *she's-been-around side*—had not only been at the establishment on the night he was there, but that she was interested in him: a gut-carrying, chubby-faced, balding fifty-four-year-old ugly son of a bitch.

She'd introduced herself as Crystal—which he doubted was her real name—and said she was in town for the night and wanted to know if he'd be interested in having a good time. Based on her hard eyes, aging flesh on her young face, the way she ran a finger along his forearm and pressed her tongue against her upper lip, he knew she was a hooker, since he'd been fucking them over the years. Of course, not in the small town of Spencer, but when he took a trip to Binghamton or Albany for that very reason.

"Hell, honey," he said, "I'd love to have a good time with you, but you're going to need to convince me you aren't a cop."

It was extremely odd that a hooker would be in Dwight's, but he'd seen stranger things.

"I ain't no cop, Mister," she said, sounding a bit annoyed. "And if you ain't familiar with what I'm asking—"

"Oh, I'm familiar all right. It's just, well, you know. I got to be sure." He looked at her, then said, "come on," and hopped off his stool.

Crystal followed him to the hallway that led to the bathrooms, the air pungent with the smell of urine and puke.

"Ugh," she said. "I don't think I can blow you here."

Howard laughed. "Just show me your tits, and then we can leave. Go to a hotel where it's clean and we can relax." He pulled out a wad of twenties. "So, you know I've got the cash."

The young woman glanced down the hall, then lifted her shirt and flashed him a perfect set of perky, B-sized puppies with a silver hoop through the left nipple. Howard's groin tingled, his penis actually stirring—and without him having taken Viagra. The sight of those young-looking tits reminded him of Kendra Souter's. He wasn't going to need to keep that image of the girl after all, because he'd be getting the real thing.

"Hot damn, girl," he said. "Sold."

As they made their way to his car, a 2012 Cadillac Touring Sedan, Crystal told him that he was her last customer, and if he wanted her for the rest of the night, that he could have her for that length of time and it would only cost him an extra hundred on top of the hundred she'd want for fucking him. Out of curiosity, he asked how much a blowjob would've been back at the bar and she said, "Fifty, and I'd swallow."

"And if I wanted to fuck you out back, behind the bar?"

"Hundred. No anal."

"Or a whole night for two-hundred?"

"Yup, and I'll do anal. But I also want a ride to the bus stop in the morning."

"Deal," he said, thinking: *Damn, this night keeps getting better and better.*

A boner-inducing idea came to mind. With his female spy-cam locker room gig over, he needed something else. It was the perfect night to start something new, like record his prostitute sessions on his handheld camera. He would tell her to wait while he cleaned up his bedroom, and then position the camera so that it was hidden, but able to record their time together.

"Since I'm paying all night for you, I think we'll skip the hotel and stay at my place. Got all the food and drink we would want."

"Sounds good to me."

Ten minutes after leaving the bar—Crystal playing with the radio the whole time and driving him mad—he turned into his driveway and felt a giddiness befall him he hadn't felt since he'd gotten a clear shot of Missy Daisy's clean-shaven snatch. He was going to fuck this hooker in so many ways and planned on paying her an extra hundred if she'd go ass to mouth where he'd unload himself.

Ready to giggle with glee, his elation fizzled out when he saw a book resting on the driveway surrounded by what looked like broken glass. Crystal was all but forgotten as he squinted to try to make out what he was seeing, but his mind was unable to figure it out. He stopped the car just short of the debris.

"Be right back," he said and exited the Cadillac.

Up close, he saw that the book was his. It was a first edition of The Old Man and the Sea. He'd paid $950.00 for it. The cover was ripped and scuffed, the spine bent. Looking up, he noticed how incredibly clean the window to his den appeared and how his vehicle's headlights did not reflect off it. All the other windows on the house appeared normal. He tried seeing into the room from where he stood, but the second-floor landing was too high.

Someone was in his house.

Howard's breath hitched in his chest. Anger flared throughout his body; his flesh heated. Fingers balled into fists. Not only had someone broken into his home, but the scumbag had ruined his stuff. Who knew what else was going on? What other damage had been caused, or was still being caused?

He needed to fix this. Take care of the asshole in his house, if the person was still there, so he could get to his night with Crystal. For a few moments, he'd forgotten about her, the prostitute's presence coming and going. Screw that. He wasn't going to let some candy-ass, piece of trash ruin his night. No way.

Taking a few deep breaths, he returned to the car, smiling.

"Is everything all right?" Crystal asked when he opened the Cadillac's door.

"Yuppers," he said and pulled the lever to pop the trunk open. "I think my nephew was here earlier and left a mess. You know how kids can be. Call me old-fashioned, but I want to make sure the place looks good. Wait right here. I'll be back lickety-split."

"You don't have to do that. Unless there's a dead body in there, I'm a sure thing, hun."

Howard chuckled. "Still, I'd like to straighten up a little. It'll only take a sec."

After gently closing the door, he headed to the trunk, grabbed his Smith and Wesson .45 and tucked it into the front of his pants. After making sure it was covered by his shirt, he closed the trunk and headed toward the house.

His skin itched with the urge to get inside and see what was going on. Itched to catch the burgling bastard and teach him a serious lesson about breaking into the wrong home.

Most people in his situation would be on the phone with the police, he imagined. They'd be afraid to enter, or nervous about having a hooker with them. Not him, though. He wasn't deciding against calling the cops because of her. No sir-ee. It wasn't like they'd know she was a hooker or that she'd offer up her occupation. The real reason for his course of action was because he wanted the criminals all to himself. His full-carry permit wasn't for nothing. The gun was only kept in the trunk of his car when he went drinking or to school, otherwise it was on him. Always concealed.

He picked up his pace as he went around the side of the house and to the backyard. Whoever was in his house—if they were still there—had most likely seen his vehicle's headlights or heard the engine and were working toward leaving. He couldn't let that happen. And the most logical place the criminals would depart from was through the back door or a rear window.

Once around the corner, he pulled out his gun and let his eyes adjust to the darker area while at the same time listening for sounds. The moon was almost full, bright, and the sky cloudless, allowing him a clear view of the broken window.

Inching up to the back door, he found that it was locked. Taking out his keys, he unlocked the door, opening it slowly. The hinges didn't make a sound. The door was old, but Howard was a maintainer. He wanted his things to last. He worked hard for them. Keeping up the house included taking care of the little things, like oiling the hinges, as well the bigger items such as the roof which he repaired every fifteen years or so. His house was paid off, and with each passing year, its value slowly rose.

With a heart that pounded against his breastbone, he stepped over the threshold and into the house. Passing the washer and dryer, he made his way to the hall that led left and right. The darkness was wall-like, impenetrable. Most likely the intruders had left or knew he was here. Light would be his ally.

Lifting his arm, he flicked the light switch to the on position. An explosion of illumination followed, flooding the hallway with intense brightness. The chalk-white walls were on fire.

Wincing, his eyes adjusted quickly, and he felt more at ease when he could see better. Now the game was definitely on. Whoever was in the house knew for certain he was home. He'd continue to turn on lights as he went. Sure, he was more of a target now, but he wanted to be able to properly aim. Once all the lights were on, if one went off, he'd know where to head.

As he made his way along the hallway, his eyes settled on the holes in the walls and the debris at his feet. Broken picture frames and chunks of sheetrock. His breathing grew more rapid, nostrils flaring. It was difficult not to sprint ahead. The people who'd trashed his house were going to pay.

When he finally reached the living room, the place partially cast in light from the hallway, his heart sank. His television was destroyed, the thing a pile of rubble. He thought about alerting whoever might be in the room, calling out that he had a gun, but decided he would rather surprise the son of a bitch with a bullet.

Standing just outside the room, he reached in and felt along the wall for the light switch. Fingers brushing against it, he flicked it up.

Light bloomed and he nearly cried out at the sight. The place was not just trashed, but obliterated. Drawing breath was difficult, as if some invisible hand were squeezing his lungs. A soft whimper escaped his lips as he grabbed onto the doorframe, the room seeming to tilt.

He was losing it. He hadn't expected such a disaster. It was as if a tornado had come through.

Fuck.

Not knowing what else to do, he bit his lip, the action an old trick. The sharp pain and the taste of his blood focused him. Pain had always been a grounder for him. Got him through tough situations.

He squeezed the gun's handle and swore under his breath. The anger he'd had came roaring back. Good. He needed it more than ever. Whoever had done this to his home was as good as dead. There'd only be police when there were bodies to report. And if no one was in his home, he'd hunt them down, kidnap them, and then blow them away inside his house.

Self fucking defense.

Tears streaked his face. He couldn't believe how upset he had become and quickly wiped the salty liquid away with his shaky hand.

He needed to explode, and for a moment feared his heart would give out because his anger was so great. But he couldn't allow that to happen. Couldn't allow himself to tense up. To react instead of act. He couldn't let the intruders know they'd gotten to him.

Taking a few deep breaths, he turned around and headed back down the hall. He was seeing red despite his efforts to calm down.

Before entering the kitchen, he smelled a mixture of food—onions, tomato sauce and pepper. Turning on the light, he tried to ready himself for what he'd see, but the sight was far worse than he could've imagined. Broken dinnerware and food were everywhere, splattered across the floor and walls as if a bomb had gone off.

No, not a bomb. It looked like an episode of Extreme Food Fight, if there was such a show.

As he stood there, mouth hanging open, a chunk of lasagna fell from where it had been stuck to the ceiling and plopped onto the floor. Closing his maw, he returned his focus to finding the intruder. Or maybe he had multiple intruders. He'd have to be more careful. Gun pointed, he scanned the area, his finger ready to pull the trigger.

Brewmeyer's thoughts returned to the hooker. She couldn't see his place like this. In a small way he hoped the vandals had left so he could take her to a hotel and screw her brains out. But he doubted that was going to happen. He was too pissed off.

His night was ruined.

No, fuck that. He was going to pound that bitch. Viagra would get him hard and he'd make her work to get him off no matter how he felt. He was going to need the release, especially if he couldn't kill the bastard or bastards who destroyed his home. But if his house was vacant, he'd leave, take care of his business with her, and then deal with his mess of a house tomorrow.

But that was getting ahead of himself. There were still rooms to check.

He moved through the kitchen, almost slipping on one of the many beverages that had been splashed about. Then there was the lasagna, the baked dish sprinkled over everything and causing havoc on his balance. It was only when he heard the crunching of ceramic and glassware that he felt like he had a grip on the floor.

Getting to the adjoining hallway that led to the rest of the house was a relief. He flipped on the light switch there. The carpet was dirtied with food from the intruder's footprints. Despite that, he wiped his shoes off on the carpet and continued forward.

When he reached the stairs leading to the second floor, he peeked into the waiting darkness and listened for sounds, then moved onward toward the den where the food-steps led.

With his back pressed against the wall, he reached around and flipped on the den's light.

Ready to blast whoever was there, Howard leapt into the den's archway.

There was no one there.

The room was intact save for one missing window. There was plenty to ruin, like the beautiful, polished cherry-wood desk with the Mac laptop resting on it. Or the collection of antique model cars that were in his glass display case. Or the shelves of rare and signed books—one book missing from its usual place, the gap glaring like the missing tooth on a smiling dentist. Then there were the paintings hanging on the walls, each one at least five-hundred dollars or more. All this meant one of two things: Either he'd interrupted the intruders as they were about to trash his den, forcing them to leave, or they were still here, hiding behind his desk.

Studying the beige carpeting, he saw a muddle of footprints and noticed how a pair led around to the front of the desk. There was no return trail. His eyes focused on the leather chair. It wasn't pushed in all the way, the way he always kept it.

Conclusion: Someone was hiding under the desk or had simply moved it.

Howard felt his gun hand slick with sweat, switched the weapon to his left hand and wiped his palm on his shirt before switching back. His pulse was quick, and he itched to send a few bullets through the desk and hopefully hit the scumbag behind it. But he held off, not wanting to ruin the piece of beautiful furniture, and because he wanted the intruder to know the fear of death, not just die.

He stepped up to the desk, ready to tell the idiot to come out, or he'd start shooting, when the floor creaked behind him. Eyes widening, he spun around and saw a grotesque figure holding a knife. Some kind of hideous, faceless mutation. His finger pressed against the trigger. He was ready to kill whatever it was, and then his brain clicked into the proper gear, and he saw that there was no grotesquerie. It was a person wearing a stocking over their face, like the psycho cult leader had worn in Stallone's Cobra, one of his favorite 80s movies.

"Don't move, dirtbag," he said, having always wanted to say such a thing. He couldn't believe it—he'd caught the scumbag. How would he have been able to do it if he didn't have a gun? Screw all those whiny liberal assholes and their anti-gun bullshit. He had a right to bear arms and bear arms he did. A law-abiding, trained gun owner was a good thing. A necessary thing. If more law-abiding citizen's carried guns, there would be a lot less crime.

People would think twice before robbing a store if half the store's customers had guns. Think twice before breaking into a home. Think twice before shooting up a campus or movie theater—because instead of ducking and hiding and running people could shoot back. Guns made the weak as strong as the strong. Guns made people of all sizes equal.

Howard was amped up and ready to shout out to the world. When the news vans showed up and cameras were shoved into his face, he'd tell the world how it was, and how a gun had saved his life.

"Drop the knife," he said.

The intruder didn't move.

"You've got two choices, dirtbag. Either drop the weapon or I drop you." After he said it, he wished he'd come up with something better, like: *Drop the knife or eat lead.* Yeah, that sounded cooler. He'd use that line for the cameras.

The knife fell from the intruder's grasp and thudded to the carpet.

"Whatcha gonna do now, partner?" Stocking Head asked.

Howard smiled and felt a gleam in his eyes. "Kill the scumbag."

CHAPTER NINE

BOBBY LOOKED AT HIS phone. He couldn't believe Daemon and Jade were going to remain in the house. What exactly did that mean? Were they planning on jumping Brewmeyer in his own home? That had to be the case. But with their masks on? They wanted an upfront reaction, to see the man's terror or anger, and then to beat the teacher down. Simple burglary and vandalism was going to turn into home invasion and assault.

Serious crimes, and those two weren't the brightest when it came to being forensically careful. Besides all that, Bobby wanted a piece of the action, especially if his ass was on the line too. He'd be implicated and have charges against him as well. If he was going to be grouped in with them, then he was going to have his share of the good time and make sure they didn't get caught.

He wondered if he should remain outside. Daemon hadn't said not to come in. Hadn't told him to wait where he was. Then again, why should he listen to Daemon when he himself was the smartest of them?

While deciding his best plan of action, he noticed that Brewmeyer exited his car and left it running with the lights on. Then as the schoolteacher went around to the back of his house, Bobby saw the metallic glint of steel appear in the man's hands.

Shit, Brewmeyer has a gun.

He quickly called Daemon again.

"What?"

"Dude, Brewmeyer's got a gun. Get out of there."

"Nah, I think we'll stay. I could use a new weapon."

"We can come back more prepared," Bobby said.

No reply.

"Daemon?" He looked at his phone and saw that the call had ended.

Damn it. He couldn't just stay where he was and hope for the best, but he also didn't want to get his ass blown away because his friends were morons. Unless Daemon had found a gun in the house... If that was the case, maybe Daemon thought he could get a jump on the guy.

The whole point of them coming to Brewmeyer's was to piss the guy off by fucking up the man's car. Now they had an opportunity to not only piss him off but beat him up. He was good with that. Brewmeyer had it coming. It hadn't been planned out, but he could make it work. Guns easily led to killing. Something like that should be planned. Strictly planned. Murder involved forensics. It was taken way more seriously than breaking and entering and assault.

A light came on in Brewmeyer's Cadillac as the door opened. A young woman stepped out and shut the door behind her. A lighter sparked to life, briefly revealing the female's pretty face before the glow of a cigarette cast her face in an eerie orange firelight.

Bobby knocked the surgical cap off his head as he ran his fingers through his long hair. Picking it up and putting it back on, he knew things were spiraling out of control. Another person entering the picture just made things more complicated. A gunshot or scream would cause the woman to call the cops.

With no more time to contemplate what to do, he made sure the surgical mask was covering the lower part of his face and headed toward the woman.

"Miss," he said as he approached her.

The young woman put a hand to her chest. "You almost scared the pee out of me, coming out of the dark like that."

Up close, the woman appeared even younger than he originally thought. A date for Brewmeyer. She was not. He didn't recognize her. She could be the man's niece or a family friend. A student looking to better her grades. Either way, she was hot.

"Sorry," Bobby said, refocusing himself. "I live a couple houses away and wanted to tell Mr. Brewmeyer that we were robbed."

"Robbed? Tonight?" She took a long drag on her cigarette.

"Yeah. While we were sleeping. They even took our cell phones. It's why I'm here, so I can use Brewmeyer's phone to call the cops. But since you're here, could I use yours?"

"Cops?" the girl asked, eyebrows raised. She shook her head. "Um. I..."

Bobby didn't understand the girl's hesitancy. "If I could just use your phone—"

"They will go to *your* house, right? Not come here?"

"Yeah..."

"Okay." She smiled, her concerned look turning to one of relief. *Weird*. She was clearly hiding something. Didn't want the cops around. But it didn't matter. All he needed to do was get her phone away from her.

When the girl turned around and went to open the car door, Bobby pulled out his folding knife. He flipped open the blade with practiced haste and wrapped his arm around her neck, before pressing the blade to her tender throat flesh.

Chapter Ten

"You ain't going to shoot me," Stocking Head said.

"Oh, sure I am," Howard said. "Going to send a sweet message to all the scumbags in the world. Break into my house and you don't leave alive."

"You're not a murderer. You're a fucking schoolteacher."

Brewmeyer's eyebrows came together. The guy knew him or had been watching him. This was no random break in. "Take off the stocking."

"Fuck you."

"You can take it off or I can pull it off your corpse."

"Guess that's what you're going to have to do, then." Stocking Head crossed his arms over his chest and stood tall.

The guy either wasn't afraid and crazy or was putting up a good front. Howard had planned on simply blowing away the intruder when he found him. But now he was curious. Besides his desire to see the bastard beg for his life before he shot him, he now wanted to see who he was dealing with. The pleasure of knowing his enemy by staring the dirtbag in the eyes and letting him know he had won would only add to his satisfaction of ridding the world of unneeded filth. However, he could find out who the intruder was after the fact. He could shoot the guy and leave the stocking on until the cops identified the person, making his surprise genuine. No, he wanted to see the low-life loser, know who he was killing.

The shitbag was tough, and it appeared the man wasn't going to budge when it came to doing as he asked. That was all right. He would simply have to show the guy how serious he was by shooting him in the leg or some other non-lethal body part.

As Brewmeyer was deciding where to put a bullet, crunching sounds came from down the hall.

Shit, someone else was in the house.

"Whoever's here, I want you to know I've got my gun trained on your partner. Try anything and he's a dead man."

Multiple footsteps approached. A whimper. Then Crystal came into view. A tall man with long hair wearing a surgical mask had a knife pressed to her throat. Her face was streaked with tears.

"Drop the gun or the bitch dies," Long Hair said.

Brewmeyer recognized the voice. His mind worked. The slender build and greasy, long hair. It was Bobby Lancaster, one of his more vile students and detention regulars. The shitbag had grabbed the hooker and come in through the back door. Disgusted, he said, "Bobby, how good to see you again. You turned out exactly as I thought you would: a complete waste of human flesh. A total loser."

The room went still, then: "Good, then you know I'll cut her."

"Please, Mister," Crystal said, "do as he says."

"Yeah, right," Howard said. "For all I know, you're in on this with them."

"No, I swear I'm not."

He saw Bobby's eyebrows knit together, clearly a look of confusion under the mask when the scumbag realized the girl was an innocent bystander. It didn't matter. He wasn't relinquishing his weapon. But now he had a new problem. A witness problem. He wouldn't be able to kill the intruders outright. He could shoot Bobby and simply say he was protecting the girl. She'd back him up on that. Or if he could let them go. Knowing one intruder was Bobby, he could easily track the loser down, and then find out who the other guy was when he tortured the long-haired freak.

"Take off the mask, Pantyhose Man," he said, figuring he'd try again before switching to plan B.

"Did you hear me, asshole?" Bobby said. The prostitute squealed as Bobby's knife-wielding arm jerked.

"Yeah, and I'm not dropping my gun. Do what you want with her. Go ahead and add murder to breaking and entering. Until your friend here takes off his mask, none of you are going anywhere."

"You want to see my face?" Stocking Head asked.

Howard recognized the voice now, not sure why it had taken him so long. He wasn't surprised. Bobby had been Daemon's shadow, the two always together. Daemon had been the worst in his class.

The air seemed to thicken with tension. Things felt as if they were about to get out of hand. Control would be lost soon if he didn't do something.

Looking at the hooker, he felt bad for her. Truthfully, he didn't want her to get hurt. In fact, he still planned on fucking her later on. She would understand why he hadn't given up his weapon. Hell, if he saved her, she'd be grateful to him. Maybe even give him a discount or fuck him for free out of gratitude.

Stocking Head pulled off his veil, the material stretching like a condom being pulled off a semi-hard penis.

"I should have known," he said, feigning ignorance. "The idiot twins together. Maybe the cops will let you share a cell."

"We ain't going to jail, asshole," Daemon said, grinning.

A floorboard beneath the carpet creaked behind Howard. Remembering how he'd originally thought someone was hiding under his desk, he spun and was met with blinding pain across the side of his head.

His finger jerked, and the gun roared just before he fell into blackness.

CHAPTER ELEVEN

From her small space below the desk, Jade pushed out the chair in half-inch intervals as the men talked. Daemon was buying her time. She wanted nothing more than to shove the chair against the wall, spring to her feet and charge Brewmeyer with her hammer held high and ready to strike. However, she stayed calm. Bobby coming in with a hostage was brilliant and only added to the room's din and chaos, making her movement less noticeable.

Before Bobby called alerting them to Brewmeyer having a gun, she'd been hiding behind curtains while Daemon hid at the top of the stairs. If they heard the man on the phone with the cops, they'd attack him with savageness, knowing they couldn't afford to take their time, and then leave out the back. But hearing that the man had a firearm, Jade thought they should leave right away. She went to head out the way they came in, assuming Brewmeyer would come in through the front door, when Daemon stopped her.

"We don't know where he is," he said. "Headlights are blasting the front of the house with light, but Bobby said Brewmeyer went around back. We need to hide and see what happens. Let him think no one's here, then we jump his ass."

"He could be on the phone with the cops," Jade said.

"Nah. If that was the case, he'd do it from the safety of his car, not while traipsing around in the dark with his gun out. We hide here and wait to hear from Bobby or take care of this shit ourselves."

"This is so fucking hot. I'm so wet, babe."

"You're my sick little slut, aren't you?"

"Yeah, I am."

They swapped spit and then separated. Daemon hid in the hall closet across from the den while she crawled under the desk. Sitting there, she bit her bottom lip out of anger. Throwing the book through the window had been reckless. Her stupid mistake might cost them prison time, or worse. If she died, so be it, but she couldn't die at the hands of her enemy. Brewmeyer must have seen the book in the driveway and noticed the missing window glass.

As horrible as the possible outlook could be, her level of excitement was something new and incredible. She was being born into something fresh, something better. And to think all this time she'd thought getting high and fucking was the best thing in the world.

Finally, after all that, here she was, sneaking up behind Brewmeyer, hammer raised, when the fucking floorboard creaked beneath her. It ruined the surprise she'd wanted to give him but went with it. Without hesitation, just as the dickhead turned around, Jade whacked the fucker's skull. The gun went off and was loud as hell, but the bullet went wide and disappeared into the wall behind her. Blood splattered the bookcase next to Brewmeyer as the gun fell from his grip. His legs gave out, and he crumbled to the floor.

Daemon moved with panther-like speed and scooped up the weapon.

Jade stood over her former teacher and raised her hammer to strike again, but noticed he wasn't moving. Blood gushed from the hole in the side of the man's head, the cream-colored carpeting turning a dark crimson. Fragments of eggshell-like bone lay beside the man. Jade marveled at the sight.

"Damn, girl, you broke his skull open," Daemon said. He bent next to the body and felt for a pulse. He shook his head. "Nope. He's a goner."

"Oh my god," Bobby's hostage shrieked. "You killed him."

"Fuck," Jade said and smashed her bloody hammer against the desk, breaking off a chunk of fine cherry wood. "I wanted that fucker to suffer."

Daemon stood and approached her. "I know, babe. But what's done is done. You saved our asses."

"But the whole reason we came here was to make him suffer. Piss him the fuck off. Screw with him. Give him a beating and make him wonder who did it." She smacked the side of her mask with a fist. "One fucking whack and he's gone. I was ripped off."

"We all were," Daemon said, nodding, his voice tender. "But fuck him. One less asshole in the world, right?"

Jade's chest heaved as she sucked in an angry breath. She shoved past Daemon, squatted over the corpse, and began smashing its head. She screamed as she pulverized the face, quickly making Brewmeyer unidentifiable. Blood splattered her entire body as pieces of flesh and bone were flung about, sticking to the walls and ceiling. Soon, there was no head, only a stump of meat, and Jade was laughing hysterically. Bobby's hostage screamed the entire time.

Daemon turned around to tell the girl to shut up when she attacked Bobby by elbowing him in the stomach and smashing her heel into his right foot. Bobby was no longer holding his knife against the girl's throat, guessing the whole crazed Jade scene had been quite the distraction. Bobby bent over and howled in pain.

The girl sprinted to the front door and was fiddling with the lock when Daemon charged after her. He raised the gun and was about to pull the trigger when his curiosity got the best of him.

Bobby rushed past him, knife in hand.

"Don't kill her," Daemon shouted.

Bobby grabbed her by her blonde locks and yanked her off her feet. He dragged her as she kicked and screamed back into the den before picking her up, wrapping an arm around her neck, and pressing the knife to her throat. She quieted immediately, but the tears continued.

"Please don't kill me," she sobbed.

Bobby walked her over to the gore-splattered couch and shoved her onto it.

Jade was standing now, her entire frontal region from face to feet covered in Brewmeyer's remains. Bits of flesh dangled from her mask, her hammer slick with blood. The carpet around her was a pool of dark, glistening crimson.

"You're a sick puppy," Bobby said.

"I feel better now," Jade said and stepped past the headless corpse, the carpeting squishing in marsh-like fashion. She stood before the girl. "Who the fuck are you?"

The girl's mouth hung open. She was shaking. She turned her head and vomited.

"Disgusting," Jade said.

Daemon told the young woman to look at him.

"I don't want to. I don't want to remember your face."

Daemon pressed the barrel of his gun against the girl's temple. "Look. At. Me."

Slowly, she turned her head and looked into his eyes. He withdrew the piece from her head and stepped back.

"I asked you a question," Jade said.

"Yeah, the lady asked you who you are," Daemon said.

"I'm nobody," the girl replied. "Just a hooker. I've been arrested multiple times for prostitution, drug possession, shoplifting, and assault and battery. Let me go." She held up a hand as if swearing on the Bible. "I won't say a thing to anyone."

"Get the fuck out of here," Jade said, swatting her thigh. "Looks like ol' Brewmeyer had a few skeletons in his closet. Self-righteous prick."

"You don't look like a hooker," Daemon said.

"I am. I swear. I work down in Binghamton. I've got my own problems and nothing to do with this. I don't like cops and don't need them in my life. My name's Crystal, by the way."

"Wow," Jade said. "So, you're, like, one of us?"

"Yeah. Exactly. I'm like you all." The girl smiled. It looked forced.

Jade looked at Daemon and then at Crystal. "And you promise not to tell on us? Or tell anyone about this whole mess?"

"She saw my and Daemon's face," Bobby said, now standing in the den's entranceway.

Jade removed her hockey mask, her face splashed with blood. "Now she saw mine too. Happy, ya big baby?"

"I don't care what you look like," Crystal said. "Even if I wanted to remember, I'm terrible with faces. Couldn't pick you out of a lineup if I wanted to. But like I said, I won't say a thing to anyone."

Jade put her hockey mask back on. "Hhhhmmmmm. What do you think we should do, fellas?"

"What's your last name?" Daemon asked Crystal.

"Potrovich. I have I.D. if you want to see it."

"Nah, we trust you. You're like us, right?"

"Yeah."

"And your address?"

Crystal gave it.

"You're far from home, Crystal."

"Yeah, I was visiting my sick grandmother. Sounds like bullshit, but it's true. She goes to sleep early, so I figured I'd go to the local watering hole and get a few drinks, then thought I might as well make some money. She pointed at the headless corpse. He was taking me home. Paid me already too, so I'm good."

"I would never sell my pussy," Jade said. "Let some strange, nasty fat fuck stick his dick in me? My mouth, cunt, and ass? No way. Especially the ass, that's for love only. I guess props to you, girl, even though you're a disgusting whore."

"What the hell are we doing?" Bobby asked. "We can't stay here all night."

"True," Daemon said. "We need to finish up and move out."

"So, do we trust her and let her go?" Jade asked, looking at Daemon as she twirled the hammer in her hand.

"I think we can trust her," Daemon said. "She's like us, after all, a misfit." He motioned for her to leave.

Jade stepped aside, and when Crystal didn't move, she said, "Well, get the fuck out of here before we change our minds."

The prostitute rose to her feet, legs shaky. Her eyes darted from Daemon to Jade, and then to Bobby, who was standing at the room's entrance. Head down, she stepped past Daemon, hesitated, and then proceeded forward, where she stopped in front of Bobby, who was blocking her way.

"Excuse me," she said, keeping her head down.

"Can't let you leave," Bobby said. His arms were at his sides, right hand gripping his knife.

Crystal looked up. "They said I could leave."

"This isn't a democracy," Bobby said.

"Looks like we have a problem," Jade said.

"How are we going to solve it?" Daemon asked. He'd been waiting for this. Letting the girl go was a test for Bobby. He needed to make sure the man was with them.

"How about she blows Bobby as payment to pass?" Jade suggested. "I love to watch live porn, even if it is Bobby's little dick."

"Fuck you," Bobby said coldly.

"What do you say, Bobby?" Daemon asked.

Bobby's shoulders rose and fell with the breath he took. Crystal's hair wavered when he exhaled. "This wasn't planned." He took a small step back, then his knife hand flashed across her neck. She staggered backward as blood spurted from the five-inch slit running across her throat. Bobby was streaked with crimson. He didn't move. Crystal turned around and looked at Daemon with accusatory eyes. A look that said, *You said I could leave.*

Daemon didn't like it and whacked her across her face with the gun, crushing her nose. She went down, twirling like a top, and crashed to the floor. He kicked her in the mouth and dislocated her jaw, the flesh drooping like a loose hanging rubberband.

Jade howled and jumped in, landing in a squatting position over the girl. Her hammer hit Crystal's broken nose square and sank into her skull. The hooker's body trembled for a moment and then went still. Lifeless eyes stared at the ceiling.

"I had to get in on that," Jade said. "Make it a sweet group kill."

"She would've died from the cut I gave her," Bobby said.

"Probably," Daemon said. "But my blow actually killed her."

"Bullshit," Jade said. "She was clearly alive and moving until I caved in her face."

"Fuck it, she's dead," Daemon said. "No worries now."

Not wanting the blade tarnished, Bobby finished wiping it off, then stuffed it into its sheath on his belt and stepped up to Daemon. "What the hell was that about? Were you really going to let her go if I didn't stop her?"

"Of course not. I just wanted her to feel like she was going to get away. Have some fun with her. By the way, was there anyone else in the car?"

"No."

"Why didn't you shut it off?"

"I had other things on my mind."

"Fair enough."

"So now what?" Jade asked, standing. "No point in trashing the rest of the place to piss off Brewmeyer."

"It would still be fun," Daemon said. "Destroying shit is always fun."

"The less time we spend here, the better," Bobby said.

"Grab some valuables and split?" Jade asked.

"No," Bobby said. "The only thing we'd take is cash, and we don't need it."

"Can we just look around a little?" Jade asked. "See if we can find some nasty shit on Brewmeyer. Maybe he was into child porn or something. We can ruin that fuck's name."

Bobby reluctantly agreed, and the house was scoured. Bobby had gone outside and shut off the car. A large safe was discovered in Brewmeyer's basement, the thing bolted to the cement floor. There was no way they were getting inside short of finding a professional thief or dynamite and the latter might not work.

"This sucks," Jade said and kicked the safe. "I want to see what's inside."

"Me too," Daemon said. "Motherfucker."

Bobby was thinking beyond valuables or child porn. He was looking for something that would lead the cops in a different direction than him and his friends. To a different town would be best. A simple home invasion would lead the locals to look close to home. Brewmeyer was an asshole and had skeletons. Who would have thought the man used prostitutes? For all he knew, the man was a killer and planning on dismembering the hooker. There was a good chance the safe did hold damning evidence.

"We might not need to open it in order to have its contents for public consumption," Bobby said.

"What's that?" Daemon asked.

"I've been thinking about all the forensic evidence we've left behind. It will be impossible to clean up. Not that our DNA is on file or anything, but once it's collected, it will be. Then if any of us are busted for something where we would be forced to give a DNA sample, we'll get linked to this crime. No statute on murder."

"So, what then?" Daemon asked.

"We burn the house to the ground. It will destroy all the DNA. Once the place is safe, the cops will go through it. They'll find the safe and open it. Anything damning inside will be newsworthy."

Jade nodded her head as if listening to music. "Yeah, I like it."

"Good thinking, man," Daemon said.

"There's more," Bobby said. "When they find the remains of the hooker, they'll figure her, and his deaths had something to do with Binghamton. Drugs. Money. Who knows? But it will cause the police to look elsewhere."

They headed to the kitchen. Daemon went to the garage and found a can of gasoline. He doused the downstairs. The burners were turned on the stove minus the flame. The hiss of gas filled the air.

On the way out, Bobby dropped a match on the gasoline saturated carpet. Fire blazed throughout the house in minutes. The trio ran into the woods and headed back the way they came, Jade giggling all the way.

PART II: AMBER

Chapter Twelve

It had been six months since Amber was raped. Officially, the forced act would have been called date rape. As far as she was concerned, date rape was a bullshit term concocted by some piece of garbage attorney to make the act of rape appear less harsh. As if getting raped by someone you knew was much better than getting raped by a stranger. Rape was rape. Plain and simple.

Amber hadn't been raped in an alley, or beaten and left with contusions, or came home to find a burglar had broken in, and then decided to rape her. She had been pledging a sorority when it happened. Her rapist was a handsome frat boy who came from money and held the position of president of his fraternity.

She had rushed a few different sororities before deciding upon the one she wanted to join, Sigma Tau Sigma. Her only hope was that they wanted her too. Two days after the sorority's mixer, she received a visit from two of Sigma Tau Sigma's sisters and was whisked off into the night where she became an official pledge.

She knew it was going to be hell, but well worth it. Her only sibling was a younger brother, and while she loved him and wouldn't trade him for the world, she had always wanted a sister, too. Joining a sorority would mean multiple sisters for life and ones she could count on. And it would be her pledge class that she would bond with the most, as they would have to band together to make it through the tough times. Yes, she'd have to endure humiliation, getting screwed with and broken down, but it would all be to be built back up again with an understanding of what it meant to be a sister and have a second family for life.

All pledges went through the same torments and rituals as the pledges that had come before them. It's how bonds were formed. Amber and her pledge class were going to have to rely on each other. They would grow close and become, as one, a single unit that worked together. That was the goal of pledging.

The first night, she'd been stripped down to her bra and underwear. Sisters from the sorority pointed and laughed. They held different colored markers and circled so-called problem areas on the pledges. As soon as Amber had been told to strip, she knew what was going to happen. Sorority and fraternity hazing rituals weren't as secret as they used to be thanks to the internet and easily shareable knowledge. But it was one thing to have read about something, to know what was coming, than to go through it. The experience had been humiliating. Thankfully, Amber regularly worked out, ate healthy foods and had the DNA of an athlete. Every part of her body seemed to be just the right size and in the right place. She was toned, had a flat tummy and a sculpted ass with a puffy fullness that filled out a pair of jeans perfectly.

Her B-sized breasts were perky and big enough for a handful, fitting her slim frame well. Her one big flaw—not that she saw it as one—was her appendix scar, the thing immediately circled with marker. Her right ass cheek, when positioned in a certain way, showed a dimple, one her last boyfriend had found cute. It was also circled. A pimple on her chin was marked, as well as a Florida-shaped birthmark, on her left hip. All in all, she made out well, especially compared to some of the other girls who had cottage cheese ass areas circled, thick thighs, pimples, scars, crooked noses and toes, stomachs that weren't perfectly flat and one girl had her mouth circled thanks to crooked teeth. Most of the pledges were pretty girls, if not average looking. Amber found it interesting, as if she was studying something for a sociology class, how her fellow pledges reacted—embarrassed and scared.

Amber was confident, and although she felt odd having people laugh at her and draw on her, she didn't feel any less of a person. She was a pretty girl, above average for sure, and she knew it. Pretty girls knew they were so, but unlike many of them, Amber didn't let it go to her head. Didn't let it make her overconfident in life. She was not conceited. By eighteen, most individuals knew where they fared in the social game. She'd dated good-looking guys, sometimes real jerks. Got whistled at by passersby at times and hit on at parties.

She also had a kind heart and looked out for the lesser socially accepted people, like the time she slapped Beatrice Miller for tripping Cindy Updike, one of the ugliest and most picked on girls in school.

College was a whole new ball game. Her previous high school status and popularity meant nothing. She was a tiny fish in a vast ocean. Joining a sorority would elevate her status quicker than if she went at it alone. It was a little narcissistic, she knew, but in the real world, after college, status would mean something. Whether a person was part of a biker gang or a law firm, they were labeled and looked at according to their job or duties. A person's rep carried a lot of weight, and joining one of the most popular sororities on campus and one that was nationally recognized would only serve to bolster her reputation.

By the time the first week of pledging was over, Amber was emotionally and physically drained. Besides college class work, she had to learn the sorority's history including the Greek alphabet, current and past members' names and where they lived, and then she and the other pledges had to do all the other extracurricular activities that came with pledging, like getting woken up in the middle of the night to get one of the sisters an order of French fries from McDonalds or a roll of paper towels from the 24 hour Walmart. Then there was the real hazing, like when she and the girls were locked in the basement and had to eat bags of Tootsie rolls until they threw up. Or were locked in a small closet and each girl had to eat an entire onion before they were let out.

The sorority had a lot of parties, or mixers, as they were called. Usually, pledges were nothing more than gofers for the sisters and their guests, and not allowed to drink.

Except for the occasional weekday—usually Thursday—parties and mixers were held on the weekend. Either the sorority would play host to one of the college's fraternities or vice versa.

Rules for pledges at parties varied slightly from event to event, but for the most part, a pledge was not allowed to speak unless spoken to. They got drinks for sisters or brothers, took out the trash, got more alcohol from the basement fridge, and cleaned up after the party was finished. Very rarely were they allowed to wear makeup or nice clothing, most of the time having to dress in oversized T-shirts with their pledge names on the front and back.

Amber, like most of the girls, felt as unattractive as ever during parties, but didn't let it get her down. She wanted to remain strong-headed and never forget herself, always making eye contact with the boy guests. It was during her last mixer that she was pleasantly surprised when Rex Warchester, the President of her sorority's brother fraternity, started talking to her and gave her permission to speak.

Rex was incredibly good-looking. No, scratch that. He was damn hot. He stood an inch over six feet, had the build of an Olympic swimmer—she'd seen him with his shirt off at a party once; six-pack of abs, pecs of armor, and python-like arms. His beautiful, brown, make-a-girl-weak-in-the-knees eyes, chiseled jawline and full lips made him the male spectacle of any party he attended.

"How do you like pledging?" he asked.

Amber felt her face flush as she straightened herself out. She tried to look him in the eyes but couldn't get past his cute dimples.

"I'm sorry," he said. "You can speak."

She blinked and came out of her daze. She never felt so shy before, and needed to remember to be confident, if not at least fake it.

"You know, harsh," she said, answering his question with a smile. "Terrible in fact." She shook her head. "But it's as I expected." Her heart was hammering away, and her palms were slick with sweat. She couldn't get over how ridiculous she felt, but guessed it was due to the fact that she wasn't wearing makeup, dressed as if she were staying home on her couch ready to eat potato chips and that the sorority had broken her—a bit. Oh, and then there was her name: Bunny.

"So, Bunny. ...." he said, tilting his head and grinning.

"Yup, that's my pledge name."

"Going to tell me how you got it?"

She rolled her eyes and said, "Cuz of my teeth and how they look when I smile, and the fact that I love carrots."

Rex laughed. "Interesting. I thought it was because you're so cute."

Amber felt her cheeks grow heated. Her smile widened as far as her muscles would allow.

"They don't look so big to me," Rex said. "I think your name was more about the carrots than anything else."

Unable to help herself, Amber giggled. She needed to get control of her emotions and stop acting like a schoolgirl with a crush. The whole process of pledging had made her this way. They wanted her to be uncomfortable. As strong-minded and confident as she thought she was, she had to admit, to a degree, that she did indeed feel like less of a person.

"My name's Amber," she said.

"Rex," Rex said, and they shook hands. "But you can call me Chaos."

"Chaos. ...." she said, nodding as if the name was all right. "And how did you get that name?"

"Because I'm so level-headed and cool. A straight shooter."

As Amber and Rex continued talking, the music grew louder. Hearing each other's words was nearly impossible, and Amber found herself shouting into Rex's ear. The brothers and sisters were getting rowdier, the drinking intensifying. The living room was a packed dance floor, and the air was smoke-filled. Shots were being shot and a funnel session was happening at the keg across the room.

"Do you want to go somewhere a little quieter?" Rex asked, his lips an inch from her ear and sending pleasurable chills throughout her body.

Yes, please. Take me up to my dorm room and put those delicious lips around my clit and make me scream your name, she thought, but instead said, "I'm really not supposed to leave the living room area except to get more drinks if needed."

"Between my frat's pledges and yours, I think the party will be fine. Besides, I'm the president of the frat. No one is going to complain, and I'll make sure you don't get in trouble. I'm sure you could use the break."

She glanced around. Every one of the sisters was busy, her fellow pledges either being told to drink or just standing around. "Um, okay. Just for a bit, I guess." Amber wasn't naïve. Rex was hoping to score. Maybe not an outright fuck, but a blow or hand job at least. He was going to be sorely disappointed if that was the case, despite how much she'd like to have a one-night stand with the stud, but that just wasn't how she did things, especially while she was pledging and especially with the fraternity's president. If they made out a little, that would be fine.

"Want a drink to take with you?" he asked. "I'll serve you for a change."

She wasn't supposed to consume alcohol tonight. If she was caught, not only would she be punished, but the rest of the pledges, too. Hell, maybe the whole situation with Rex was a setup. A test. No, she didn't think so. If a member of a fraternity or sorority told her to drink, she had to obey. Do whatever was in reason.

"Well, if you're telling me to drink. .." she said, biting her lip.

"Yes, I am." He held up a finger. "Be right back."

Rex returned a minute later with two red cups of beer and handed her one before telling her to follow him. They left the living room and traveled along a hallway, and then up a winding staircase to a landing above. A few people were waiting in line for the bathroom. Though the floor trembled from the music below, she was able to talk without raising her voice. Rex's room was at the end of the hall. As he pulled out a set of keys and unlocked the door, Amber glanced into her cup and saw that it was already half empty. She'd been guzzling as they walked, needing the alcohol to calm her nerves. When the door was unlocked, Rex pushed it open and gestured for her to enter. She said thank you and went inside.

Rex's room was orderly, not the frat room she thought it would be. The closet door was closed. A queen-sized bed was neatly made. Posters of bikini and lingerie clad women hung on the walls among fraternity plaques, paddles, and other memorabilia. A mini fridge rested next to the couch that was in front of a large window with the shades drawn. He told her to have a seat and that he'd be right back and left the room.

Sitting on the couch, she was buzzing from the beer she drank. Another two gulps and her cup was empty. She was no lightweight. A good buzz was perfect. She could keep her wits about her while feeling much more comfortable. Hopefully, she and Chaos could make out a little. She'd even let him feel her up. But that would be it. She wasn't going to be another notch on his bedpost or some typical sorority skank. Fooling around was fine, and if she was horny later, she knew how to take care of herself. If he was really interested in her and they hit it off, then hopefully something meaningful would come of their meeting. Dating the president could take her a long way and help her in rising through the sorority's ranks. Maybe even snatch herself a long-term relationship with a real hot guy who also happened to be marriage material.

Oh, Amber. You're being an idiot now. Control your thoughts.

By the time Rex returned, Amber was really feeling the alcohol. She'd drank plenty of times before, and knew one cup wasn't enough to floor her, but maybe her empty stomach proved grounds for how fucked up she was feeling. She needed to stay in control, but decided to go with it because it would wear off quickly. It was just an initial blast, and then she'd level out.

Rex sat next to her and asked if she was feeling okay.

"Yeah, I just drank too fast on an empty stomach."

He leaned in and ran his fingers through her long, golden hair. "You're beautiful, you know that?" His hand came around and gently rubbed against her cheek.

Chills tingled her flesh, and she couldn't help but giggle. Shaking her head, she said, "You must be drunk or need glasses. I look ugly."

"Don't do that," he said. "You're really pretty. A natural beauty."

He inched closer and she could smell Peach Schnapps on his breath. His lips looked delicious, full and moist. She wanted to press hers against them. Their eyes met. Silence filled the space between them. A wordless connection was made. They leaned in and lips met. Then mouths opened and tongues explored, though Amber was having a difficult time controlling hers, as if it wouldn't quite do what she wanted it to. Rex's hand slid around her and up to her neck, where he gripped her passionately. Hot breath escaped out of her nostrils. Her crotch grew wet. She was hot for him.

His hands moved from her neck to her sides and then to her breasts. She didn't mind and let him continue. He then slid them down and went under her shirt. They traveled up her stomach, fingers creeping into her bra and finding her erect nipples. Damn, she was horny, but at the same time, felt confused. Her thoughts were foggy. Her lips and tongue were sloppy. She had even less control over them. Her body grew heavy, and it was difficult to remain upright, yet she wasn't tired.

Her arms went up. He was pulling off her shirt. She tried to stop him, but her arms wouldn't cooperate. "N. .... No. P.. .pl. .. ease. Stop."

After removing her shirt, he flung it to the floor and was fiddling with her bra. A moment later, it was off, and her breasts freed. She tried pushing him away but could barely move. Her strength was gone. "St ... op." Her voice was weak, too.

"Don't worry, Bunny. It's going to be good. You're the lucky one I chose. They'll all be so jealous."

He scooped her off the couch and over to his bed, where he tossed her onto it. "My princess." He pulled off her shoes, socks, and sweatpants. Amber tried calling out for help, but her words were meaningless whispers.

She couldn't believe what was happening, her thoughts clear. The asshole had drugged her. All the stories she'd heard, the Lifetime movies she'd watched. .... She was going to be a statistic. She had always been so careful at parties, never taking a drink from a stranger or leaving her drink unattended. How could this be happening?

She opened her mouth to scream. Nothing. Moving was impossible. But she couldn't give up.

His fingers curled around her underwear, and she felt them sliding down, her pubic hair region fully revealed. Once they were off, he sniffed them before dropping them to the floor. Looking down at her, he said, "Nice and neat. I like a girl who keeps herself trimmed." He unbuckled his belt and let his jeans and boxers fall to the floor, revealing a large, crooked, thick and hard penis. He stroked it a couple of times and then climbed onto the bed. "You're going to love this."

CHAPTER THIRTEEN

WHEN HER ATTACKER WAS finished, he climbed off Amber, grabbed a few paper towels and wiped his seed off her stomach before tossing everything into his trash bin. He then got dressed and left the room. She lay there naked and cold, tears streaking the sides of her face. Control had been coming back to her little by little. Eventually, she sat up and then got to her feet, but her head was woozy. As the room spun, she sat back down. Her body ached from head to toe. She wanted nothing more than to put her clothes back on but didn't want to risk falling and hurting herself.

She felt so fucking vulnerable. Clothing would help. But she couldn't rush it.

Then the nausea hit, seeming to come out of nowhere. Holding onto the bedcovers, she leaned over and a stream of golden-brown vomit escaped her lips and splattered the carpet. As she wiped away the spittle using the back of her hand, the door flew open. Big Bird, the sorority's vice president, entered and was followed by two pledges, Dopey and Lollipop.

"What the hell is this?" Big Bird asked.

Dopey had a hand covering her mouth. Lollipop stared at Amber with unblinking eyes.

Amber was still nauseous and feeling somewhat numb, and now she could add embarrassed. Weakly, she held a hand over her breasts and cupped her crotch as she sat. Her head was still foggy, thinking difficult, but not impossible.

"You disappear," Big Bird said, "come up here, get drunk and fuck the frat's president? Who the hell do you think you are?"

"I. .. I. .. He raped me," she managed, and tears flowed.

"What?" Dopey asked.

Big Bird's narrow, but pretty face went slack.

"He drugged me," Amber said.

"Shit," Big Bird said and ran a hand over her dark, auburn-colored hair.

"Oh my God," Dopey said, a hand still covering her mouth.

"We have to tell someone," Lollipop said.

"Just wait a minute," Big Bird said. "I need to talk to Turtle." She headed to the door, opened it, and turned around. "You two stay with her. Get her dressed and wait until I come back." Big Bird shook her head and left, closing the door behind her.

Amber didn't know what to do and remained seated. Dopey and Lollipop gathered her clothes and brought them over to her. She felt the hardness of her cell phone and something in her mind clicked. She needed to call the cops. They needed to collect evidence. Pulling out her cell phone, she pressed 9, then 1, and then the phone was swiped out of her hand by Dopey.

"What are you doing?" Lollipop asked.

"We were told not to do anything until Big Bird returns," Dopey said.

"Give me back my phone," Amber demanded, feeling more of her strength return with her anger.

The door opened. Big Bird rushed in, followed by Turtle, the sorority president. Amber didn't move. As the two women approached her, Turtle stopped and eyed the puke. She shook her head in obvious disgust and stepped around it. "What the hell is going on, Amber?"

"I want my phone back." Amber reached out, felt like she might fall, and stopped herself.

"Okay, you'll get it back soon enough, but first tell me what happened," Turtle said.

Amber couldn't believe what was happening. Someone should be on the phone with the police while the others were chasing down and beating the shit out of Rex. Clawing his skin. Supporting her. She may not be a sister yet, but she was on her way to becoming one. "That animal drugged and raped me," she said.

"Are you sure?" Turtle asked.

Amber's brow furrowed as her jaw hung loose. "He. Raped. Me." She said it as clear and as slow as possible, her own words making the situation more real than ever for her.

Turtle took a step backward and looked at Big Bird. "That fucking asshole."

"You believe her?" Big Bird asked.

"I don't know what to believe at this point, but this is a disaster. Do you know what will happen to us? To the frat, too? We'll be put under a microscope. Placed on probation. Maybe lose our charter, have a letter taken away."

Again, Amber was floored by what she was hearing. It was as if she was the star of some after-school special. These people didn't give a shit about her, only their precious sorority.

"You stink like booze," Big Bird said to Amber. "There are no marks on you. It'll be your word against his. People saw you two come in here. You need to think this through before you make a decision you regret."

"Give me my phone."

"Did you hear me?" Big Bird looked ready to throttle her. "This will go public. Everyone will know your business. The sorority will be torn apart. Your past will be on display in the news and in court, should it even go that far."

"I have nothing to hide."

"You need to think—"

"Fuck the sorority," Amber screamed. "That pig raped me!" She got to her feet.

Lollipop had tears streaming down her cheeks. Turtle and Big Bird wore masks of shock before Big Bird's eyes narrowed. "Look you little—"

"Amber," Turtle said, stepping up and pushing Big Bird back. "We understand you're upset." She put a hand to her chest. "I get it. But we'd like to deal with this internally. We take care of our own. Believe me. Big Bird is right. You really need to think long and hard about this and what it'll do to your legacy. We'll take care of you. Make sure that bastard pays. We'll get him booted out as president, maybe even the frat. He won't come to our mixers. He's rich and we'll make sure he pays you something. I mean, haven't you seen cases like this? The victim is always made to look bad. Don't do that to yourself."

Big Bird was standing with her arms crossed over her chest. She huffed, turned and headed out of the room.

Amber wanted to explode. It didn't matter what these people said. She had been raped. Violated in the worst way. Tricked. Drugged. And the motherfucker hadn't even worn a condom. She could have a disease. Have one of his evil little swimmers working its way toward one of her eggs despite his pulling out and spewing his seed all over her stomach—which reminded her that she needed to get those semen-covered paper towels out of the trash bin before she left.

Looking down, she was still naked, only covered by the small pile of clothing on her lap. She couldn't figure out why she hadn't put her clothes on yet, and guessed she was in shock despite being able to think and reason somewhat clearly.

As much as she wanted to call the police, she knew she had a long, rough road ahead of her. Worrying about that now was a waste of time. The facts were that she had been violated. Drugged, so she could not fight back. Her rapist hadn't even given her that. He was worse than a street rapist. A true, calculating monster. He needed to go to prison. Have his name splashed across every social media site.

But she also knew Turtle and Big Bird were right. Rex would have lawyers and investigators digging apart her past. Maybe find the people she'd slept with to spill details. Get them to say how she was a party girl. A total slut. They'd bring up the time she had been caught shoplifting at the age of thirteen. Her friends dared her. She was young and stupid. Though it happened when she was thirteen, she didn't doubt the record would be discovered. The whole trial would be a *'he said, she said'* event. With his high-powered lawyers, the truth might never come out. She could come away looking like a liar, or like someone looking to get a quick buck.

Screw that. No one was going to treat her like a piece of trash. Let the Internet know all about her. Screw what happened to the college and its fraternities and sororities. This was her life, and she needed to protect others from the frat boy named Chaos.

The door flew open and banged against the wall, knocking a plaque free. Rex rushed into the room with Big Bird in tow.

"You lying little bitch," Rex said.

"Get him away from me," Amber screamed. Suddenly, her nakedness was overwhelmingly apparent. She began dressing, never wanting the monster to see her naked again. She knew it would have been best to remain without clothes until the cops arrived, but she couldn't stand to be unclothed for another moment, especially in front of HIM.

"You wanted it," Rex said, pointing at her. "Hell, you were all over my shit. Attacked me." He threw his arms up. "I can't believe you're pulling this crap."

Damn, the guy was a good actor. Maybe the only way she'd ever get retribution was if she killed him.

"Turtle," Rex said, "you can't let her do this. She'll ruin my name. You know I'd never do what she's saying I did."

Amber finished dressing. "You can't even say it, can you, pig? You raped me." She turned to Dopey and held out her hand. "Give me my goddamn phone."

"What phone?" Rex asked.

"She wants to call the police," Big Bird said.

Amber lunged for her phone, but Big Bird pushed her aside and grabbed it herself before handing it to Rex.

Infuriated with revulsion, Amber growled and tried to take back her phone, but Rex shoved her away. She flew back, her foot coming down in cold vomit, causing her to slip and hit the floor.

"I bet the real reason she wants her phone," Rex said, "is because she recorded us fucking on it. It'll reveal the truth."

"Yeah, she's trying to destroy evidence," Big Bird said.

Amber hadn't gotten up yet, the blow from the fall a jarring one.

"Let me do you a favor, Bunny the Lying Slut," Rex said and threw the phone across the room where it collided into the wall and broke apart.

"What the hell, Rex?" Turtle said. "That could've helped you."

"I don't need my sex life broadcasted over the Internet or in front of a D.A. The truth is: she ain't going to do anything because she's a liar. She only wants money."

Amber finally got to her feet; the ass of her pants soaked through with her vomit. Regardless, she was fuming at how no one was sticking up for her and attacked Rex. She clawed at his face, her nails gouging four crevices along his cheek.

"Cunt," Rex shouted and threw her to the ground.

Amber sprang back to her feet with feline agility, fingers out like claws, and went to attack him again when Big Bird slapped her across her face.

"Get out of here, Rex," Big Bird said and wrapped up Amber in a bear hug. The rapist left, slamming the door behind him.

"Guys, I don't think I should be here," Lollipop said. "I'm just a pledge."

"You're going to be a sister, and this is a good thing to see, so you'll know how to handle it," Big Bird said as Amber swore and struggled to break free. "Stop it, Bunny. This isn't doing us any good."

Like a match being snuffed out, the fight left Amber. She slumped in the vice president's arms. The tall sister then released her, and she crumbled to the floor. There, she cried and cried and cried. The only thing she heard was Big Bird complaining about getting puke on her, and then nothing. What had happened to her finally hit her, the blow was like a sledgehammer. She didn't open her eyes for some time, hoping that when she did, the room would be empty. But when she finally looked around again, Big Bird and Turtle were still there. The others were gone.

"Look, this sucks," Turtle said, squatting in front of her. "But we want you with us. We picked you because we believe in you. Believe that you'll always look out for us, and we'll always look out for you. We can't allow anything to jeopardize what we have. To destroy what our former sisters have built. There can be no dark clouds over our family. Can you understand that?"

"We'll give you all the support you need," Big Bird said, sounding supportive for the first time. "Make sure that prick is removed as president and stays away from our pledges."

Amber could not believe what she was hearing. The whole evening had to be a nightmare. These girls were sick. Pathetic and selfish. She couldn't have been the only girl Rex raped. There had to be other victims. She wondered what would happen if she spoke out. Would any of the sisters back her story? Say nothing? Or worse, contradict her? Support whatever story Rex told?

"Has this happened to any other girls?" Amber asked, and the look in Big Bird's eyes told her all she needed to know. Turtle's face was blank, as usual. She was such a sweet, Southern belle of a girl most of the time. The sorority president seemed so undecided, weak and clueless. Amber wondered how the girl came to own the position in the first place.

Because Big Bird is the muscle, a voice inside her said. *She's the enforcer. The real power. Turtle is only the face.*

"I don't understand," Amber said. "Why are you protecting him? Allowing him to rape your fellow sisters?"

"We're not," Turtle said. "We're protecting you and this sorority."

"Really, we are," Big Bird said, placing a hand on Amber's shoulder. "We're here for you. Now, let's get you back to the sorority house where we can get you into a hot bath. Best place to start, I would think. To relax."

"Relax?" Amber asked, laughing, unable to stop. She wasn't sure why everything was suddenly so damn funny. There was no getting through to these girls, these so-called human beings. No reasoning with them.

When she calmed down, she saw the two girls staring at her, concerned looks on their faces. They probably thought she'd gone insane.

Maybe you have.

"Guess I'm on my own," Amber said and headed for the door.

"Where are you going?" Big Bird asked.

"Campus police."

"Pledge Bunny," Big Bird said. "Get your ass back here right now."

Amber stopped and looked back. "Or what, you going to try to stop me?" When neither girl said a thing, she opened the door and left.

Chapter Fourteen

On some form of autopilot, Amber marched through the frat house. She ignored the stares of the onlookers, despite feeling their eyes on her like scurrying cockroaches crawling over her flesh. Surely not everyone knew what had happened. Regardless, she despised them all. No one had come to her aid or defense. That rapist pig had blamed her and would make her life hell on campus. Give her a horrible rep.

She wondered what he was thinking. If he was afraid of what she'd say. Or if she would simply go away and do nothing.

Never!

She'd never forget.

Never let him get away with it.

And she was going to make sure everyone knew he was a rapist and a coward.

After leaving the frat house, she headed across campus to the security office. She would have preferred alerting the police right away, but with no phone and no one to borrow one from, she had no way to do so. But that was okay. Campus police would call the authorities. An officer or two would be sent, and then take her to the hospital so a rape kit could be administered.

She hoped Rex's DNA was still present under her fingernails from when she'd scratched him, and on her flesh where he had ejaculated, and if it wasn't, then as disturbing as it might be, she hoped some of his come was still inside her. Pre-come and all that jazz. "Boys leak, you know," her mother had told her once. "Gotta always have them wear a condom."

Along with his DNA, she prayed for vaginal tearing. The more evidence, the better her case would be. But it wasn't likely. He'd been gentle at first, invading her slowly. Not knowing how rapists thought, she guessed he had hoped to avoid bruising her in the event she went to the cops.

You were quite moist down there, remember? The voice in her head said. *And his DNA? It's probably in you alright, ready to bond with your egg and make a child. You'll have a rapist's baby. A rapist's baby. A rapist's baby.*

Amber stopped right outside the security office's entrance and shuddered. The thoughts running through her head—this other voice—was terrifying. She'd always had an inner voice, something she supposed everyone had, but it was nothing like the voice she had been hearing since she'd been raped.

It's just a symptom of what you went through, she told herself, and then pulled open the door to the security office.

Bright fluorescent light pierced her eyes like millions of tiny daggers. Squinting, she raised her hand up to her eyebrows to shield herself.

"Yes, Miss, may I help you?" a deep voice asked.

Unable to see properly—*from the drugs you were given, they made you sensitive to light*—Amber approached the counter. A large, burly man with a full but neatly trimmed beard stared at her. He wore a black and gray golf T with a matching ball cap that stated he was security. The name tag on his shirt read Officer Sherman.

"Miss, are you all right?" Officer Sherman asked.

Words escaped her. She wanted to scream that no, she wasn't all right, but something strange was happening inside her. The ability to speak was gone. Her face grew hot. She wondered if she was having a panic attack but had never experienced one before and had nothing to compare it to.

Or maybe you're feeling shame. Embarrassment for being so foolish with that son of a bitch. For letting him dupe you. It's what rape victims feel, isn't it? Like it was their fault? That they have something to feel ashamed about?

"No, shut up!"

"Excuse me?" Officer Sherman said, snapping Amber out of her inner-ness.

"Sorry, I wasn't talking to you," she said, her eyes becoming more accustomed to the bright lights.

She wasn't right yet though, and she needed to be. She needed her anger back. Needed the despise and hatred she had for Rex. No, not only for Rex, but for those fucking bitches—Turtle, Dopey, Lollipop and especially Big Bird. Fuck them all. But fuck Rex the most.

YOU DID FUCK HIM, STUPID.

No, I didn't. Stop saying awful things.

Talking to herself in her mind was, to put it simply, scary. But if she needed to do it, she would. Maybe it was the best way her mind knew how to deal with what had happened to her.

The security guard was staring at her. But fuck him, too. She was working something out.

Rex had to pay.

Yes, he does. What do you want to do to him?

Slowly cut off his penis using a rusty, dull metal nail file, she thought.

That sounds awesome.

Then I'd pluck each testicle off with pliers and listen to his screams. Watch him say how sorry he was and have him admit what he did. Make him beg for me to stop, which was more than he allowed me to do.

"Miss, I'm going to ask—"

"I was raped," she blurted, nostrils flared, hot breath coming forth like a dragon's. "I was raped. Raped. Raped." She was breathing fast now and on the verge of a mental breakdown.

The man's eyebrows rose.

"Don't look so surprised," Amber shouted and slapped the countertop. "I'm sure plenty of girls have been raped on this campus before."

"Miss, I need you to calm down." He held out his meaty hands.

Amber sucked in a long breath. "I'm sorry. I just. .... Could you please call the police for me?"

"When did the alleged rape occur?"

"There's nothing to allege. It happened."

"Okay, what time did it happen?"

"About an hour ago." She really wasn't sure how much time had passed.

The man chewed on his lower lip. He appeared to be studying her.

"What?"

"You don't look like you were just raped."

Amber's jaw fell. She stared at him. "I don't look like I was just raped? What the hell does that mean?"

"You smell like a brewery, and I see no signs of a struggle. No scratches, bruises, and no ripped clothing. Your hair isn't even messed up."

Amber shook her head. "Am I in some kind of idiot land?"

"Calm down."

"Fuck you. I was just raped. Raped. Did you hear me, asshole? Do you understand what happened to me? I shouldn't need to come in here and get the third degree from you. Treated like I'm some liar. Now pick up your fucking phone and call the cops."

Officer Sherman sighed, then came around the counter.

Amber took a step back.

"I'm not going to hurt you." He motioned to the couch behind her. "Please, have a seat. There are a few things I need to go over with you before I call the cops."

"Like what?"

"Please. Sit."

Amber went over to the couch and plopped onto it. "This is ridiculous."

Sherman sat a cushion away, his fingers intertwined on his lap. "I realize you are hurting and upset. It's completely understandable."

Amber was ready to explode. First, the girls didn't help her. Now this guy was treating her like—

Like a lying whore.

"I'm not a lying whore," Amber said.

"I never said you were," the security guard said.

Amber flinched, confused for a moment. She refocused on the security officer. "You're acting like someone stole my lunch money." She sprang to her feet and hurried over to the counter. "Hello? Is anyone back there?"

"There's no one else here."

"Then I'll wait until someone shows up."

The guy went on talking, and as much as she didn't want to listen, she did. He repeated many of the things Big Bird had said. Everything she was hearing was that it was going to be a long, almost impossible task to get Rex convicted. And even if he was arrested, he'd be released the next day. If he was found innocent and she went around claiming he raped her, she'd have a defamation suit on her hands. Security guard Sherman said he knew Rex. The spoiled brat had lawyers up the wazoo and had used them more than a couple of times to get him out of trouble. What that trouble was the man didn't say. But everyone that had messed with him paid the price and wound up the loser. The kid was bad news and best to keep away from.

Amber didn't care about any of what she had heard. She only wanted to know one thing. "How many times has he been accused of rape?"

"None that I know of."

"I'm the first?" Amber asked in disbelief.

"Yup."

It couldn't be true. Not for someone like Rex. He was clearly a planner. A devious fucker who deserved what he had coming. Her anger increased at the thought of the uphill battle ahead. She should have done more when she was in the room. Scratching him wasn't enough. She should have really tried to attack him, trash his room. Burn it down.

But then you wouldn't look like a victim, would you?

No, she wouldn't, she knew.

And you forgot to take the come-drenched paper towels. So, you better hope you don't taint or lose whatever DNA is under your nails.

"Damn it."

"Miss, are you with me?" Security Guard Sherman asked.

She'd gone somewhere again. Down a road that she knew would lead to Losing-it-ville. She couldn't allow that to happen. Couldn't let Rex have power over her.

Taking deep breaths, she said, "I'm with you." Then added, "I'm fine, too," though she was far from it.

The security guard stood and went back to his post behind the counter. "Forget about all that stuff I talked about. What matters is you, and are you really prepared to take the stand in a trial and be made out to be a dirty, money-grubbing slut? Have his team of investigators dig up your past? They'll drag your name through the mud until your name is nothing but trouble. It's happened to others, and you can bet it'll happen to you. The best thing you can do is move on. Stay away from the wealthy prick."

As quickly as Amber's rage had come to a boil, it faded like a bad dream. She had heard too much of the same thing, as if she were the crazy one. Was she wrong about wanting to go to the police? Would it be a huge mistake? She didn't think so. Big Bird and Turtle had their reasons, but what was the security guard's? Was he truly looking out for her? Had he seen this happen so many times before? Or was he hoping to avoid a school scandal? He'd said she'd been the first to claim rape, but that had to be a lie.

For the first time since her rape, Amber had doubt about going to the police. She wondered if they would try to talk her out of pressing charges once they heard the situation. It certainly didn't seem likely, but she also didn't think it was likely that she'd be raped tonight.

Besides what you've seen on television and in movies—like your precious Lifetime channel shit—what do you really know about going to court and proving rape? Aren't women always made to look like lying whores? Sure, sometimes they win a case, but that's only because it's a goddamn movie. In real life, YOUR LIFE, they lose. You'll be laughed at, never hired, spit on, and have to move far away where no one knows you. You'll either be the victim or the liar for the rest of your life. You can't win even if you do win.

Amber closed her eyes. She wanted to scream and wondered why was she talking to herself like this. She needed to be strong.

Your parents will know you're a slut. Your entire family will know. What will they think? Your friends will abandon you. The ones that stay will always look at you with pity.

"Fuck!"

Frustration filled Amber. Her hands became fists. She needed to explode, to hit something that would break. She wasn't breathing. Then she exhaled and let out a groan. Focusing, she saw the guard, his expression one of concern. Her legs were shaking. A light-headedness was coming over her. The guard moved out of her field of vision. The room was disappearing. Her legs suddenly weren't there anymore, and she collapsed.

Someone caught her before she hit the floor. Looking up, she saw Security Guard Sherman's face.

Her strength returned as if she'd been shot with adrenaline. "Let go of me NOW!" Amber struggled away as the man helped her to an upright position. Free of his grasp, she stared at him. The man had his hands out defensively. Suddenly, she realized it was too warm in the office. She had to get outside.

"I'm sorry," she said and bolted for the door.

"Miss, where are you going?"

She ignored him until she reached the door, then held up her right arm and extended her middle finger. After a second or two, she pushed open the door and left.

Cool night air washed over her. The relief wasn't as great as she'd hoped for, but she'd take it. With her mind reeling, her thoughts a jumbled mess, she meandered like a zombie back to her dorm room.

Her strength was sapped by the time she reached her door, and she hoped her roommate wasn't home. Alone time was essential. She couldn't take talking to anyone right now.

Reaching for her key, she saw that the doorknob had been busted; the thing dented and loose. Laying a palm against the thick wood, she pushed it open. The room was dark, but she was able to see papers on the floor and a container of lipstick. Reaching along the wall on her left, she found the light switch and flipped it up.

Light bloomed in front of her, and she lost her breath. With bulging eyes, she stepped fully into the room. Her laptop had been smashed, the sleek device now a pile of broken plastic and metal on her desk. Papers were strewn about the place like confetti after a parade, along with her makeup, pens, shoes with the heels snapped off and most of her clothing, the articles shredded. *Fuck Delta Omega Delta* had been spray-painted across the wall above her bed. Her roommate's side of the room was untouched.

She stood there with a hand on the wall, baffled. Someone had obviously trashed her stuff, but why had they written something derogatory about the sorority? Could the two issues be separate? Did they dislike her because she got in and they hadn't?

Thinking about it, she wondered if, like the security guard, her sorority really was looking out for her. Maybe they really did know best. She was going to need to talk to someone about it. Need support. Hell, for all she knew, they'd all been raped by Rex.

Yeah, that's it. It's a sick and twisted initiation. The Raped-By-Rex Hazing ritual. What better way to unite a group of spoiled-ass bitches?

"You're right," she said to herself. "That's ridiculous."

"Excuse me," a male voice said from behind her.

Amber jumped and spun around, claws out and ready to attack. A stocky Asian man wearing campus security attire stood a few feet away. His name tag read Lou Chang. Another security guard stood next to him, only he was at least two feet taller and wore no name plate.

"Do you live here?" Lou asked.

She nodded, still trying to catch her breath. As she stared from Chang to the tall man, she wondered why campus security was at her door. She hadn't called them. Maybe Officer Sherman had sent them to check on her or to take her statement and cover his ass.

YOU NEVER TOLD HIM YOUR NAME, STUPID! OR WHICH DORM YOU LIVED IN.

"Shit."

"Excuse me, Miss?" Officer Chang said.

"Sorry, I wasn't talking to you."

"Look, I don't know what's going on, but we received a call about someone acting crazy and in distress."

"Acting crazy? No. .... Yeah." Her words sounded far away.

"Are you feeling okay, Miss?"

"My name's Amber. And I'm just dandy. Can't you tell? I was raped tonight. No fuss." She showed her arms and neck. "No bruising, physical anyway. What more could a rape victim ask for?"

Hearing her own words scared her, but it needed to be said. Maybe putting it how she had would garner her some attention.

"Mind if we come in?" Tall asked.

Hadn't they heard what she said? Why did they want to come in? For what reason other than to —

Be alone with you.

Stop it, whoever you are, she thought, hoping to quiet The Voice.

Maybe you're a rapist attractor. Men can't control themselves around you. From now on, you're going to have to be alert and always, always be around other people. Especially around other women.

No, that wasn't right. Amber knew better, despite what The Voice had said. Her mind was fucked up, and she needed to make sure she didn't listen to it. The Voice was scary, but it was her, some inner demon that had broken through because of her tragic experience. That's all.

Her room had been vandalized. That's why they were there. Someone had heard her room being trashed.

"My room was trashed," she said, and then stepped aside and let them enter.

That had been the beginning of the end for Amber's college career. The sorority had gotten behind Rex and said Amber had been drunk and coming onto him the night of the supposed rape. It was said that Amber had been smitten with Rex for some time, and it was only after the two had hooked up that she found out he was only interested in the one-night stand. That's when she flipped out and said she would get her revenge on him by claiming he had raped her. When she found out that the sorority would not back her story, she tried to get them in trouble by trashing her own room and blaming it on them. Thanks to a witness, Amber's credibility was crushed.

With Rex and the sorority girls having the same story, Amber was made to appear like a scorned and crazy woman. After speaking with a lawyer, Amber was informed that she could still press charges, but more than likely nothing would come of it except for defamation charges brought against her by Rex.

Amber also had to pay for the damage to her room, was suspended and put on behavioral probation. Word spread quickly around campus. She became a pariah in days. Faculty and students from all grades knew her thanks to social media. She was constantly harassed by strangers, but especially by sorority and fraternity members.

Unable to deal with the unending flurry of negativity and failing most of her classes, she left school. She informed her parents of her decision, saying that college just wasn't right for her. Thankfully, the school was a four-hour drive away and no one from her town discovered what had happened to her. Her parents didn't understand it when she said she wanted to work, save up and take some time on deciding what her future held, but they respected her decision. She was able to get a waitressing job thirty minutes away from her house in the town of Ithaca.

She often thought about telling her parents everything but could never do it. Nothing good would come of it, and she'd only become a spectacle in her own home. They would push her to press charges, not understanding everything that was involved—all the bullshit lies against her. None of it mattered. Not really. The moment she showered after the rape was the moment her case went down the drain. Sometimes it was best to leave the past in the past, no matter how horrible it was, and move forward.

As difficult as it was, she moved on, taking it one day at a time. She focused on work and on her younger brother, Jason. The two were close despite their age difference. His being different—a bit odd to be specific—and extremely bright made her love him even more.

Chapter Fifteen

WHEN AMBER CAME HOME from college, Jason could tell something was wrong with her. She hadn't said anything in particular to him, but she didn't have to. Besides hearing her crying at night, she had a sadness about her. Her normally bright eyes were dull despite her smile, the same type of smile his mom produced when she had a headache and had to deal with a stranger at the grocery store or some kind of technician that came to the house to take care of one thing or another. Or like when she forced a smile every time his dad made a joke.

A week's time had passed before he finally saw her genuine smile. A little bit of light shone back in her eyes. It was when he finished building his remote-controlled drone and was ready to launch it. They had gone outside together. Amber laughed with him as it flew into the air.

At his present age of eleven-years-old, Jason could read body language and get a sense of a person's mood. This was truer for females, especially teenagers. He guessed it was due to his being close to his sister and her friends. But besides first-hand accounts, he'd loved to read and did so about the opposite gender, wanting to understand his sister further, like how female emotions could be at their most erratic during their menstrual cycles. At first, he'd thought that was the reason for Amber's distraught and faux appearance, but quickly came to realize that was not the case. To put it simply, she looked off. Somehow older. Wounded.

He wasn't one to shy away from family—but strangers, yes—so he came right out and asked her if something was wrong. "Adult girl stuff, that's all," she said. He didn't pry, but he also didn't believe her. Hadn't believed her when she told their mom and dad why she left school. Amber had been an 'A' student for the most part and had been looking forward to going to college since tenth grade. He wasn't equipped to handle such problems, if they were indeed adult female related, so he let it go and decided to do what he could to cheer her up.

He did things like ask her for help—even though he didn't need it—and get advice on social issues with classmates—stuff he truly didn't quite grasp—like when Barry Stewart asked if he could cheat off him. Of course, Jason didn't want him to, but also didn't want to come off in a negative way and be bullied. Amber told him to go to his teacher, tell him to make sure no one cheated off him. He didn't give a name. When Barry was caught looking, the teacher told Barry to keep his eyes on his own paper. Barry wasn't the wiser to Jason's informing the teacher, and that was that.

As if Jason wasn't socially awkward enough, he had skipped two grades, making him even more out of place. Other students either made fun of him or ignored him. He was never invited to parties for either being too young, too nerdy, too awkward or just plain old not fitting in. Normally, this would lead a kid down the road to a tough life and depression, but Jason dealt with it fine. He found most people boring and simple and didn't like them much. He cared about learning and building things like his drone.

Whenever he did get down and even when he wasn't, Amber always reminded him how special he was and that he was going to do great things one day. Amber understood him, unlike most others. The only reason he came up with for this was love. It had to be because she loved him. Love was intangible, highly misunderstood, and the most powerful force on the planet. He came to this conclusion because Amber was as normal as a person could be. She wasn't stupid. She was smart, but not overly so. Not like him. She was slightly above average smart in the range of most of her friends. She liked fashion, partying, boys, and doing well in school. So, it had to be love as to the reason she wanted to be around him, as well as understand him.

Love was the reason families protected their own, no matter what they came up against. It explained why a mother and father believed their child was the best and why, if it came down to it, their child should live over another. Why a parent would choose to save their single son or daughter rather than an entire city. When he thought about that, he didn't quite get it. It seemed the logical thing to do would be to save the entire city over a single person. But love wasn't logical. And though he didn't understand love or how it existed or formed, unless it was some kind of chemical mixture made up in the body, he was glad for love.

Chapter Sixteen

Killing had sparked something in Daemon. In all of them. The group's dark side had emerged, and it felt good. Whether it would have come from hanging out in the wrong place at the wrong time, drunk driving, drugs or a straight up bar fight, Daemon had always known he'd be responsible for ending someone's life. How some people knew they were destined for greatness. He knew he was destined to be bad, maybe even evil. The prevailing sense had scared him, but at the same time excited him.

Jade had been on the same course since the age of twelve when she pocketed lipstick from Walmart. When the guard confronted her, she kicked him in the balls and tried to run but was nabbed, regardless. She was like Daemon, only crazier. A hot-headed firecracker with no sense of remorse for anyone but Daemon. He was her only connection to love. She understood it because of him and would never let him go. After finding such a treasure, such a drug, she knew she could never do without him. Life wouldn't be worth much, if anything. It made her weak, and she hated herself for it, but the emotion was too strong to kill, so she accepted it, also accepting that they were one. If Daemon died, she would, too.

They were born free and, unlike most people, were able to detach themselves from society's norms. The rules had never applied to them, and when they killed those men in the SUV, Brewmeyer and the hooker, Daemon knew Jade had felt what he felt. It wasn't simply the act of causing those men's deaths, but the fact that they would strike fear into the people of the town, and that brought a feeling of god-like power that was unattainable elsewhere.

Bobby had been Daemon's best friend since they met. The two had been through thick and thin, but Daemon hadn't known if the man was capable of outright killing. Ready to move to the next level. It was why he let the hooker go. He was testing Bobby and wanted to see what the kid would do. Bobby was a bad dude and enjoyed breaking the law, but murder was something else. For a few moments that night, as the girl walked toward the den's exit, Daemon was nervous. If Bobby hadn't killed her, Daemon would have had to. Then he'd have to kill Bobby and leave his corpse in the house for the cops to find. It wouldn't have been identifiable, but through dental records due to the charred state.

Sure, it had been Bobby's idea to burn down the house, but Daemon was sure he or Jade would have eventually come up with the notion. Bobby would've then been blamed for killing the prostitute and Brewmeyer. Daemon was glad it hadn't gone that way. Because from that point onward, whoever wasn't with Daemon was against him.

But all that nonsense was behind him. Bobby was one of them, and he was grateful to have his friend alongside him and Jade.

Killing had been fun. Burning down Brewmeyer's house was the cherry on top. Subsequently, time seemed to crawl. The hard part after such fun was the lying low and waiting. Getting a taste of taking a life and then having to stop was difficult. It amazed Daemon how a simple, juvenile game of mailbox baseball could turn into something far more thrilling and satisfying.

The trio of killers was eager to begin another round, but understood patience was going to be necessary. The cops were on the lookout and spending all their time investigating the murders. Local and national news had come to town the day after the murderous attacks. The grisly crime scene was a complete shock to the town. It was awesome. The cops were clueless.

Speculation ran rampant. Brewmeyer's reputation as a straight shooter and pillar of the community was ruined after the prostitute's remains were identified and her profession revealed. The cops changed their focus to Binghamton where the woman was from, thinking a pimp, jealous client or drug dealer had killed her and Brewmeyer. The teacher had simply been in the wrong place at the wrong time with the wrong person.

The trio paid attention to the news, listened to the police scanner, and got wasted. Daemon's Toyota was stripped of the Plasti-Dip, despite there being no report of his car being spotted near the scene. Daemon was the only one with a job and kept going to work despite not needing to. Bobby had enough money for them all, but he didn't want to rely on anyone but himself, and it was best to remain as usual. Give the police no reason to suspect a thing in the event they somehow came around.

Bobby was certain any and all evidence left behind in the house had been destroyed by the fire. He was the brains of the group. He was the cool nerd, always interested in learning. Knowledge was power for some, and he was a master at it. There had been plenty of smart killers throughout history, and Bobby was going to be another.

"Taking lives is natural," he said. "There will always be a variety of people, and all are needed for a society to work, including its killers. They are a part of the DNA of civilization, of human culture. All societies have had and still have them. Without good, there is no evil. Without crime, there would be no police. Whether it is for fear's sake, a natural order of population control, just in our DNA, from damaged brain cells, or an evil force within our souls, killers are part of the world."

Bobby didn't feel bad or good about killing. He was only doing what was inside him, what felt right. There were too many people on the planet anyway, too many assholes, and he would be glad to be rid of them. But he also knew that a real killer just killed whoever was in front of them when it was time to kill. But how to decide who lives and dies? This was the question Bobby had posed to himself and then the group. The game would decide, and it would be fair. As long as people died, he would feel he was doing what he was put on the earth to do. Together, the trio had become what society pushed them to be. Classmates, strangers, teachers and all the rest had been a necessary part of getting the trio to realize who they were. And now that they did, the town was going to know true fear.

CHAPTER SEVENTEEN

THREE WEEKS HAD PASSED since the events at Brewmeyer's and the murderous trio was as confident as ever.

"I told you we had nothing to worry about," Bobby said as he lay back on the beach chair beside the pool. "We were careful, and that, my friends, is the key to getting away with illegal shit."

"Careful?" Jade asked, sitting up in her chair. "We fucking torched everything. And we got lucky with the hooker."

"We got lucky with her because of my diligence. It was my idea to burn the place down, remember? Simple idea—yes. But I came up with it."

Jade huffed, blowing a few strands of her purple hair out of her eyes. "You want props for the idea?" She slowly clapped her hands. "Con-fucking-gratulations."

Bobby shook his head. "Unappreciative bitch."

Jade laughed. "That's right, asshole, but you know I still love you, Robert."

"I want a gun," Daemon said. He leaned back in his chair, threw his feet on the table, and lit a cigarette.

"What for?" Bobby asked.

Daemon looked at him and frowned.

"We've got the shotgun."

"I want a .45 or .357 Magnum. Something powerful I can carry around. Keep hidden."

"That's the kind of shit that will get you in trouble. Bullets can be traced. Shotgun blasts can't."

"Well, I'll chance it. We'll want more than a short-range scattergun if the shit hits the fan, like if we need to escape a situation or to just protect ourselves."

"No, we don't. That's cheating. The game needs to have rules, or what's the point?"

"Not for the game, dude. For protection and assurance if things go wrong. Don't you get that?"

"We'll get more shotguns. They'll work better if we use slugs. Fucking things will be more powerful than any handgun you can get your paws on."

"I need something I can conceal on my person, man."

"I know you'll do what you want, but this *is* a joint venture and I say it isn't a good idea to start carrying around illegally gotten firearms."

"You really are a worrywart," Jade said, lighting a joint. "I want a gun, too."

"I'm going to keep us out of prison, that is, if you listen to me."

"And what happens if the cops are after us?" Jade asked. "Like if one day during the game things go wrong? If it's us going to prison or us killing as many cops as we can, those piggies are going down. We'll need to out-gun those motherfuckers if we want to get away."

Silence.

"What, nothing?" Jade asked.

"I'm done with this conversation," Bobby said.

"Good. We get guns then."

Bobby exhaled and ran his fingers through his long hair. "Fine, but we can't use them or carry them around unless we're playing the game. And if we do shoot someone, prepare to dig out the bullet and make it impossible for forensics to identify the caliber."

"Oooh, dissection," Jade said, blowing out a plume of smoke. "Might be fun. A shitload more entertaining than those frogs I cut up in biology."

"We'll head over to Dirk's tomorrow," Daemon said and took the joint from Jade as his cigarette smoldered in the ashtray.

"Did you all forget about the lying low part of our plan?" Bobby asked. "We sit quietly for at least a month before the new game begins."

Daemon pulled on the joint, the coals burning brightly even under the afternoon sun. He handed the joint back to Jade and exhaled a moment later. "Going to Dirk's has nothing to do with Brewmeyer's. Two separate issues. Hell, if we don't go, the cops might think something's up with us."

Jade laughed and stomped her feet. "Yeah, true. You did say we should act normal, Bobby."

"You really want to buy a gun from that tweaker?" Bobby asked.

"Do you know anyone else close by who we can sort of trust?"

"No, but that asshat will squeal if he's ever pressed by the cops. He's cooking meth and selling heroin. That shit's federal, and it's only a matter of time before he's busted. He's fried his mind over the last few years using his own product."

"Don't worry about that," Daemon said, crushing out his cigarette butt. "If you don't want to come, then stay here."

"Don't be ridiculous. If you guys are going, I'm going. We're in this together, and I don't trust that meth-head."

"That's what I want to hear. Because we're a fucking team and teams stick together."

Chapter Eighteen

They drove over to Dirk's place the next day. The meth-head lived in a dilapidated house that looked ready to crumble at any moment. It had missing sections of siding, appeared to be slightly slanted as if the foundation or ground were giving way, and multiple antennas on the roof, most of which were bent at odd angles. Where there were sections of siding, the at-one-time white color was now sun-faded and gray with grime.

The abode was concealed from the road by a thick forest. Daemon drove his Camry along the quarter mile dirt road and took his time, the numerous ruts and potholes causing the vehicle to bottom out on occasion. When the house came into view, he parked a good hundred yards away.

Dirk owned over two hundred acres of land, mostly wooded, but the house rested on a three-acre section of clearing where only grass grew. A dented and sun-faded Subaru Forester was parked in front of the house. Sitting in the car port alongside the dwelling was a rusted brown pickup truck with its hood raised.

Dirk inherited the property from his grandmother—who had raised him—after she passed away five years ago. He'd gotten offers to sell and offers to rent from Fracking companies but had refused them all. Instead, he used the two-hundred acres to hide his methamphetamine-producing lab.

After parking the car, Daemon and Jade got out. Bobby climbed into the driver's seat. The car was kept running. Dirk had been known to be jumpy upon receiving uninvited guests, especially if the man was high. If need be, they'd be ready to roll out quickly.

As Daemon and Jade approached the porch, the front door flew open. Dirk leaped out, shotgun in hand. His eyes were wide and cracked with red. Daemon saw the barrel point at him and he stopped. Dirk's long brown hair looked like it hadn't seen a shower in weeks, the stringy mop like oiled strings of yarn. He'd gotten skinnier since the last time Daemon had seen him. He wore a multi-stained wife beater and blue jeans with more holes than a spaghetti strainer. Both articles of clothing appeared too large for the normally muscled man.

"Is that how you greet an old friend?" Daemon asked, holding his hands partially up.

Dirk jerked the shotgun and fired a round into the air before setting its sights back on Daemon. "Now I see you, Daemon Winters. Hot damn. And your pretty lady, dressed to impress. Nipples hard, too. Guess my big old gun here isn't that scary, huh, little lady?"

"I love guns, little man," Jade said, arms lowering.

"I didn't tell you to put your hands down," Dirk said.

"You never told us to put them up, either."

Dirk laughed. "You's a funny little cunt, ain't you?"

"Dirk, can we talk business now?" Daemon asked.

"Shit, so this ain't no social call?"

"We can make it both if you'd like. So, how you doing?"

"I'm doing good. Real good. Dirky boy's always doing good."

"Glad to hear it, man."

Dirk pursed his lips and appeared to be thinking, but the shotgun remained pointed at Daemon. "Hmmm. Haven't seen you since.............

Tired of waiting, Daemon said, "Since we ran into each other at the Big M."

"Nope," Dirk said, shaking his head, still appearing deep in thought.

Daemon sighed and wondered what bullshit scenario the man was going to come up with. The last time he'd seen Dirk really had been at the Big M supermarket. It was an easy time to remember because the meth-head's penis had been hanging free through the unzipped pair of jeans he was wearing.

It was right before closing and the store was practically empty of customers. Dirk had gone to embrace him in a brotherly hug when Daemon noticed the man's penis flopping about as he approached. Daemon held out a stiff-arm and kept him away, saying he was coming down with a cold and didn't want to infect anyone. Two barely dressed skanks had been with Dirk, one flanked on each side of him. Both females—one bleached blonde, the other scarlet red—were clearly cranked out of their minds, smiling like idiots and giggling.

The blonde's right breast was hanging out of her black halter top, but she didn't seem to care. She grabbed Dirk's penis and led him away, saying how she hadn't gotten a chance to finish him off yet. The other woman, Marcy Redber, was someone Daemon had banged a few times in the past. She asked him if he'd like to party, and when he declined, she snorted like a pig, squeezed her tits, turned around, farted, and caught up with her friends. Daemon couldn't believe how low the bitch had sunk.

"No, you're right," Dirk finally said. "It was at the Big M, and I was really fucked up."

"I hardly noticed," Daemon said. "I was pretty shit-faced myself."

Dirk lowered the shotgun so that it hung at his side. "So, what brings you by?"

"Looking to buy a few guns."

"Something for a cunt too," Jade said.

Dirk guffawed as he rubbed his chin. "Why don't you two come on in and we'll chat some?" The man turned around and headed back inside, letting the screen door slam shut behind him.

Daemon looked at Jade, who shrugged. "Hope I don't catch anything," she said.

The two walked forward, up the rickety stairs, and into the house.

The air was rank with the odor of sex, weed, and excrement. After a few inhalations, Daemon's mouth felt like it was coated in some awful film. Jade's face scrunched up as she let loose a sound of disgust. Empty beer and soda cans littered the floor and living room table, along with razors, magazines and pipes.

A naked woman with tattoos covering her chest, arms and thighs lay on the stained and torn leather couch. Her nose, eyebrows and ears contained hoop-shaped piercings, and each of her nipples had a thick bar through it. Her legs clearly hadn't been shaved in some time, the hairs like a layer of fuzz, and her bush sprouted up like the head of a huge broccoli floret. She looked at Jade and then at Daemon, giving them a weak smile and a wave. "Come to party?"

"Not today," Daemon said, wondering what the hell Dirk was doing with all his money. The guy had to be making a killing off his product. What was the point of having such an illegally lucrative business that could send you away for a long time when you lived like a sewer rat? Might as well go on welfare. The drugs had really fucked up the man.

As he and Jade stepped farther into the residence, the front door closed behind them. Spinning around, Daemon saw Dirk step up to Jade and press the barrel of the shotgun against her head.

"Now tell me why you're really here," Dirk said.

"What the fuck are you doing, Dirk?" Daemon asked.

"You with the cops? Working for the man?" Dirk looked like he hadn't slept in days.

Nostrils flared, Daemon said, "Hell no. You know me, Dirk. C'mon. Put the gun down."

"Yeah, Dirky boy," Jade said and withdrew a knife from the front of her jeans. "Put the gun down. We're here to do business."

Daemon caught her eye and slightly shook his head.

"Cops. Feds. They all trying to catch me. Take Dirk down."

"They'll never take you down, baby," the girl on the couch said, laughing.

"We ain't the cops, asshole," Jade said through gritted teeth.

"You two get busted for something?" Dirk asked. "Turn snitch?"

Daemon clenched his fists and jaw. Dirk was too far gone to deal with. Smoked way too much of his own product. He figured dealing with the man would be annoying, but not to the present degree. Unexpected was the word of the day.

"Take off your clothes," Dirk said.

"What?" Jade said.

"Not you. Your man. I want to make sure he ain't wired."

Daemon went to lift his shirt when Dirk flinched and pressed the gun harder against Jade's head, causing her to wince. "Nice and slow."

Daemon grabbed the bottom of his Megadeth T-shirt and lifted it to his chin, revealing his ripped abs. "See, no wire."

"Take off your pants."

Daemon released his shirt.

"Do it now or your woman here loses her pretty little head."

Jade's eyes became slits. Her chest heaved with each angry breath. She wasn't scared, as hard as that was to believe. She was pissed. Daemon's own chest swelled with pride. His woman was indeed awesome. He also wanted to keep her a lot longer and decided he needed to get past this crazy shit as soon as possible without Jade or himself getting hurt or killed.

"Okay, I'm taking off my pants." He popped the button free and then lowered the zipper. The jeans fell around his ankles.

Dirk smiled. "A tightie-whitey man like me."

"I like to keep my junk in place."

"Yeah. I get it."

"Can I get dressed now?"

"Sure, man," Dirk said, keeping his gun trained against Jade's head.

Daemon pulled up his pants. "We're all good now?"

"Not until I check your woman."

"Touch me and you die," Jade said.

Taking his hand off the shotgun's forestock but leaving the weapon pressed against Jade's head with a finger on the trigger, he poked her in her arm using his index finger. "Oh, look, I'm still breathing. Don't you know the man with the gun is the boss?"

"Enough of this shit, Dirk," Daemon said, beginning to lose his cool. "You know me. If you don't want to sell us weapons, then we'll leave."

"People change," Dirk said, his voice cold. "They get desperate. They even get taken by aliens and returned to spy for them."

Daemon knew at that moment that there was no hope of the transaction going smoothly. He saw a glint of light reflect off the blade of Jade's knife and knew if this didn't end soon, she'd react.

"Did you hear about that house fire over on the other side of town, where two bodies were found?" Jade asked.

"Yeah. Fucking pigs stopped by and asked if I knew anything about it."

"That was us. We killed Brewmeyer and the hooker he was with. Then torched the place."

"That was you guys?" Dirk said.

Daemon noticed how the meth-head's shoulders seemed to relax. A genuine look of surprise was on the man's face. "Yeah, that was us."

"Why?" Dirk asked.

Daemon lied, explaining how they had wanted revenge after Brewmeyer ratted them out for selling weed. They wanted to trash his house, but he came home. "Things happened and Brewmeyer wound up dead. The hooker was collateral damage."

Dirk nodded. "Damn, you guys are crazy motherfuckers."

"So, you see, we ain't working for the cops," Jade said. "We need guns in case the hooker's people come for us." She attempted to step forward. Dirk flinched and moved with her like a shadow. "Don't even think about doing that again, girlie."

Jade groaned. "This is such bullshit."

"How the fuck do I know if you're telling the truth? Maybe you got busted for killing Brewmeyer and are working for the cops to lessen your sentence." He leaned closer to Jade's ear. "Now strip, so we can get on with business."

Jade made eye contact with Daemon. He shook his head. Her nostrils flared. She closed her eyes as if taking a moment to calm down, opened them, and slipped the knife back into her pocket. She lifted her tank top, revealing her black bra, pierced belly button and the totem pole of severed heads tattoo that ran up her side.

"Turn slowly around," Dirk said and stepped back.

Jade stared down the barrel of the shotgun. Dirk eyed her torso, then told her to remove her shorts. "Or I can reach down there and check for myself."

Jade let go of her shirt, then slid her frayed jean shorts down around her black Timberlands. She wore matching thong underwear. Daemon's penis stirred as he looked at her. The sight of his woman's puffy, tight ass and the dagger tattoo above her crack was sexy as hell. He couldn't believe he was turned on by the scene. The next time they fucked, there would have to be gunplay.

"Turn around," Dirk said.

The meth-head's voice shook Daemon from his daydream. Anger surfaced as his skin grew heated. This perv was only doing this to get a peek at Jade. "Enough of this shit. You can see she ain't wearing a wire."

"It's okay, babe," Jade said and turned around in place, arms up and out.

"Damn, you is fine, girlie," Dirk said.

"Thank you. Now can I get dressed?"

"Y—yeah. Go ahead." Dirk lowered the shotgun.

Daemon exhaled.

Jade bent, grabbed her shorts, and pulled them up.

"Now that I know—" Dirk began when Jade's arm shot out and flashed in front of his throat. A long slit appeared in his flesh a moment before blood gushed from the wound. The shotgun boomed, and a hole appeared in the floor. Dirk let go of the weapon and clutched it to his throat as he staggered into the door. His hands, arms and white tank top were slick with glistening crimson.

Splattered with blood, Jade pointed to her knife and laughed. "You fucking disgusting idiot. How do you like my ass now?"

Dirk gargled something unintelligible as he continued to claw at his throat.

Daemon picked up the shotgun.

The woman on the couch was crying. "You hurt my Dirky. Fucking bas-tards." Her face contorted into a mask of rage. She bent forward and reached under the cushion. Half a second later, she pulled out a steak knife and jumped off the couch. Jade was still laughing and pointing at the dying man, unaware of her attacker. Daemon raised the shotgun, pumped a round into the chamber and fired. A basketball-sized hole appeared in the charging woman's chest; her left breast gone. She spun to the ground with a flop only to spring back up, knife still in hand.

Eyes wide open, she stumbled forward as Daemon racked another round and fired. Her jaw vanished in a spray of blood as the buckshot tore through bone and muscle. Teeth were shattered and embedded into the wall. The jawless woman's legs gave out, and she went down.

Laying a foot in front of Daemon, she pushed herself up and crawled for-ward, her tongue dangling free and scraping the floor. Jade turned her attention to Daemon's victim. Still laughing, she said, "Holy shit, you turned her into a fucking zombie. Better shoot her in her head."

Daemon thought his girl was the sexiest thing all covered in blood. He couldn't have asked for a better woman. He racked the shotgun again and was happy to find another shell. He wanted to blast the woman's head completely off. Pressing the barrel against her skull, he pulled the trigger and disintegrated her head. Brain, skull, and flesh flew in all directions, leaving only a pulpy mess of hair.

"Wow, that was one tough bitch," Jade said.

"This sure didn't go as planned."

Jade turned her attention back to Dirk, who was still alive. She walked up to him and stuck her knife into his eye socket. His legs spasmed and then fell still. "Fucking guy wouldn't die." She pulled the knife out and wiped off the blade. "Fuck this shit-bag. He thought he could get a cheap look at my goods without consequences?" She snorted, coughed up a loogie and launched it onto the corpse's rat-like face.

Daemon couldn't believe it. She was more pissed about being told to strip down to her throng than having a shotgun pointed at her head.

Despite things turning ugly fast, truth be told, they had planned on killing Dirk once they had his weapons. Any witness to their criminal activities needed to die. Then there was also the need to murder. Bobby seemed much more in control of his desire to kill. Daemon guessed it was because he feared getting caught more than he or Jade did. But that was a good thing. As long as they made sure to always kill together, their chances of getting busted were greatly reduced. And Bobby had been down with killing Dirk too, but only after the guns had been acquired.

Events didn't always go as planned. Now that Dirk was dead, they'd have to search the man's house for weapons. If the firearms weren't there, they'd have to go elsewhere.

But they had killed again. It felt wonderful. The grisly fashion of taking life was euphoric in a way that was new and made a drug high seem like a sugar rush. Killing was the adult version of getting that new toy he'd been waiting so long for.

Something banged against the front door. Dirk's corpse slumped to the side from the impact. Daemon pumped a round into the gun's chamber and aimed at the door. Jade stood ready with her knife. The door boomed again before flying open, sending Dirk's body into the wall behind it. Bobby was there, shotgun in his hands.

"You moron, you almost got your head blown off," Daemon said.

Bobby stepped inside and looked around. He stared at the headless woman. "What the hell happened?"

"Things didn't go as planned."

"Wonderful," Bobby said, resting the shotgun on his shoulder.

"Hey, Dirk was a jerk, and he had to go," Jade said as she shoved the knife back into her shorts pocket.

"Where is he?" Bobby asked.

"Behind the door," Jade said.

Bobby pulled the door away from the wall and looked behind it. "Oh, so that's why it was so hard to open."

"Everything's good here," Daemon said. "Go back outside and keep an eye out."

"Fuck you," Bobby said. "I get to kill whoever's next. We can use this to our advantage. Tie it to Brewmeyer." Make it look like a drug thing for sure."

"Whatever," Daemon said. "I just want to find the guns."

"Well, don't take too long. We don't need someone showing up and making things more complicated. It isn't like Dirk doesn't get visitors."

"Right."

Bobby left. Jade cleaned the blood off her as best she could, leaving the towel she used in the center of the room. They searched the house, stepping on pizza boxes, over overflowing litter boxes and tossing items aside. The couch was moved. A hide was located in the floor under the rug, the space filled with bags of meth. They left it and moved to the kitchen, then the spare room, where a stained mattress lay next to a desk with a computer on it. Jade quickly looked through it and found numerous records of Dirk's drug business. It hadn't been updated in weeks, leading Daemon to believe at one time Dirk had been all right in the head. His own product had ruined his mind, and it was only a matter of time before someone took him out. Jade made short work of the laptop, smashing it to pieces.

Next, they went into the bedroom and were almost afraid to touch anything. Hypodermic needles rested on the nightstand next to overflowing ashtrays. The walls were dented and scuffed as if ongoing wrestling matches occurred. Various colored stains dotted the sheets and carpeting, the shaggy flooring appearing as if it had never been vacuumed. The closet was a mess of men's and women's clothing, both hung up and on the floor.

From there, they found the crawlspace, pulled down the ladder, and went up. The air was rank and smelled like death. Jade couldn't deal with it and returned downstairs. Daemon breathed through his mouth, and when he pulled the lightbulb string, the place bloomed into view. A long-dead raccoon, shriveled and eyeless, lay a few feet away in a steel trap. Boxes towered all around. Searching each one would take time, time they didn't have.

Daemon would have to pick a few, then move on. The plan was to burn the place to the ground if anything went wrong—and things had clearly gone wrong. There could not be any evidence of their presence. Daemon wasn't going to be one of those criminals who spent most of his life in prison.

After finding nothing but junk in the first four boxes, he could no longer take the stench and left the attic, but not before finding a crowbar.

Downstairs, he and Jade destroyed everything in their path. Sure, they could have just burned the place down and left, but it was too much fun smashing stuff and they'd hoped to find where the weapons were hidden. They even ripped open the walls, hoping Dirk had stashed his weapons there, but all they discovered was mold and sheetrock dust.

When they were finished, they stood in the living room.

"Too bad we weren't into drugs," Jade said. "We'd have hit the gold mine."

"Yeah, too bad. .." Daemon said frustrated, then threw the crowbar at the flat screen where it embedded itself.

"Feel better, babe?"

"Fuck no. I'm pissed as hell. We need guns and the gun seller is dead."

Jade came over and pressed herself against him. She licked his lips, and when he went to kiss her back, she stopped him. Using her left hand, she unbuttoned his jeans, then slid down the zipper. "Seeing you in action really turned me on. I want you. Now."

Daemon's cock stiffened as Jade's hand rubbed the shaft. "We're supposed to be leaving soon."

"A quick fuck among the corpses and I'll be your sex slave forever," Jade said.

"You're my sex slave now, woman."

She slapped him.

He smiled, then spun her around and yanked down her shorts. He pulled her panties' string to the side and shoved his hardness between her lips, rubbed the head up and down with slickness before entering her from behind. She moaned as he thrust. He grabbed her hair and pulled as he rammed into her. She begged him to make her come.

A few minutes later, they exploded together, and then as he pulled out, the sound of an approaching vehicle entered his ears.

Chapter Nineteen

Bobby was growing incredibly warm and bored. Trickles of sweat tickled his spine. Normally, he'd have the air-conditioning running and a game going on his cell but having taken the battery out of the phone to keep his location private, and needing to hear if a vehicle was approaching, those options were out. He had the latest Hunter Shea novel with him but hadn't opened it yet. It really didn't matter what he had brought along with him.

He was the lookout and needed to keep his mind focused on his surroundings and his ears on the police scanner. The novel kept calling to him. He never should have brought it with him. It was a constant distraction. With things already having gone off track, he knew he couldn't afford to take his mind elsewhere. Getting out and stretching his legs wasn't even an option because he needed to remain ready to leave.

If he was like Daemon or Jade, he could smoke cigarettes to help pass the time, but smoking tobacco was simply idiotic, and smoking a joint was out of the question for anyone in the position of lookout.

Turning the key in the ignition so that the power came on, but the engine remained off, he checked the time and saw that an hour had passed since he'd gone inside. They were taking too long. Dirk's place may be out in the middle of nowhere, but he was a dealer of illegal items. People came and went at all hours. Hanging around wasn't a good idea.

He couldn't believe how quickly Daemon and Jade had already screwed things up. Then again, sending two hotheads to do a deal with a paranoid meth-head had been a recipe for disaster from the start.

With both car windows down and no breeze, he had to keep fanning himself with one of Daemon's CDs, the man still buying them because he liked owning a physical object of his music collection. "If the file-cloud goes under, man," Daemon said one night while they were getting high, "I won't give a shit. All you MP3 assholes will have to buy all your shit again." Bobby had tried explaining how that wouldn't happen but gave up after Daemon said old school ruled and wouldn't stop chanting it for ten annoying minutes.

Reaching into the back seat where the small cooler rested on the floor and held a few sodas, he heard the rumble of an engine. Knowing the road was a quarter mile away and the fact that the sound was getting louder, he knew they were getting visitors.

He froze for a moment before jumping into the back of the car, yanked down the seatback and crawled into the scalding trunk. The air was like an invisible wool blanket wrapping itself around him, squeezing. Breathing was difficult as sweat poured off him, stinging his eyes.

Ignoring the unpleasantness, he returned the seatback to its normal position, and then grabbed the shotgun. He found the gun slit and opened it, allowing him a clear view of the house and front yard.

The approaching vehicle grew louder. The Camry shook, and then he saw the large black pickup truck pull into view. The tires were three times the size of normal tires, and the windows were as pitch black as the paint job. Two men hung in the back, holding onto the light bar. One was tall with long hair and an equally long beard; the other had a bald dome and lacked any facial hair. Tattoos covered both men's arms.

The pickup parked alongside the house a few feet from the porch. The men jumped down as the passenger door opened. Long-beard had a handgun tucked into the waistband of his pants at the small of his back. Baldie had a knife strapped to his boot. A slender woman exited from the passenger side. She wore high heels, leather pants and a pink bikini top that was bursting with boob. Atop her head was a pink-dyed beehive hairdo. A line-backer of a man got out of the driver's side. He wore all black sunglasses and a cowboy hat. The woman stretched, letting out a loud, obnoxious yawn. Cowboy Hat came around to the front of the pickup.

"Whose piece of shit is that?" he asked, pointing at the Camry.

"Never seen it here before, boss," Long-beard said.

"No one else was supposed to be here," Cowboy said. "Check it out."

Long-beard moseyed toward the Camry and disappeared from Bobby's sight for a minute before reappearing around the other side. "No one's in it."

Cowboy surveyed the area. "Keep an eye out."

Long-beard returned to the pickup and stood next to Baldie as Cowboy and Bikini Top walked up the porch stairs and to the front door. Cowboy wrapped his knuckles on the door. "Dirk, you in there?"

Bobby closed his eyes for a moment.

This was bad. Really bad. Of all the days for people to show ...... The visitors weren't the run-of-the-mill dime bag buyers either. They appeared to be purchasers of large quantities. Bobby had been around enough low-life druggies to know the difference.

Bobby could probably take out two of them, maybe even three, depending on how prepared they were when under fire, and how fast he could cock his weapon and fire it. Most likely, he'd wind up taking a bullet or two.

There was also the chance that when Dirk didn't show, they would leave. But that didn't matter. They couldn't be allowed to leave; not after having seen Daemon's Camry and possibly remembering its license plate number.

Having no choice, Bobby reached into his pocket and withdrew his cell phone and battery. He popped the power source in and turned on the device. It seemed to take unusually long for the thing to boot up, but when it did, he sent a text message to Daemon's phone.

While waiting for a reply, he cooked in the trunk. Sweat lined his flesh, and every breath was nauseating. Impatience boiled within his bones, the need for fresh air like heroin to a junkie who hadn't fixed in days. Strong-minded, he needed to be. Keep his cool, despite the heat.

Staring at his phone, the object, now a shadowy shape in his hand, sweat stung his eye. He wiped it away, cleaned off his forehead with his shirt, and cursed under his breath for the phone to ring. If events turned sour when they were separated, the plan called for cell phones to be turned on so they could communicate via text messages. For all Bobby knew, Daemon and Jade were fucking in the attic and unaware of what was going on. There was no way he could remain in the trunk for hours if the visitors decided to wait around.

Cowboy was pounding at the door now and calling for Dirk to answer.

"Drove all the way out here, you fuckwad," he said. "You best be in there."

"Guy's probably at the cookhouse," Bikini Top said.

"Wouldn't that be just great?" Cowboy said.

"Want us to go get him, boss?" Baldie asked.

"Sure, go take a few hours and traipse across his two-hundred acres of thick woods, oh, unless you know where the fuck it is?"

"No, I don't. I just thought—"

"I know what *you* thought. It's how you operate ......Not thinking things through."

"Idiot," Long-beard said and swatted the guy upside his head.

"We'll wait right here until he gets back," Cowboy said and took a seat on one of the porch chairs.

Bobby's phone lit up as it vibrated, letting him know he had a message.

Daemon: Plan?

Bobby: They aren't leaving, and we can't let them. They may have seen your license plate. Find guns?"

Daemon: Got one.

Bobby: Good, cuz they are armed, but I think we can take them.

Daemon: Let's do this.

Bobby: Wait for my signal. Then come out shooting.

Bobby clicked off the phone and took the battery out, placing the items in his pocket. Taking a deep breath, he quietly said, "Here we go," and then banged on the trunk. "Help!" He pumped a round into the shotgun's chamber. "Help. Get me out of here." He stared through the gun slit and saw all eyes were on the Camry.

"What the hell?" Bikini asked.

Long-beard and Baldie whipped out their guns.

Bobby banged again. "Hey. Is someone out there? I'm in the trunk."

Cowboy shook his head in disbelief as he came down the porch stairs. "Get that fucking moron out of there."

Baldie and Long-beard looked at each other and laughed. As they headed toward the car, they tucked their guns back into their pants.

"Where's the keys?" Long-beard asked.

"In here with me," Bobby replied and took aim through the slit, keeping the barrel just inside the trunk. He braced himself as much as possible for the ringing his ears were going to feel, knowing it wouldn't matter. He pulled the trigger with his sweat-slicked finger. The gun roared and jumped in his hands. Baldie's crotch vanished in a spray of fabric, flesh and blood that decorated the grass behind him.

Bobby pulled the trunk latch and sprang up.

Long-beard was reaching for the gun tucked into his pants.

Bobby pumped the shotgun, sending a spent shell onto the lawn and a loaded one into the chamber. He raised the weapon and saw the gun Long-beard was going for drop to the ground. Bobby fired and blew a gaping hole into the man's stomach. He was thrown back a few feet, where he crashed to the ground.

Bikini Top was screaming and ran behind the pickup. Cowboy was nowhere to be seen.

The front door of the house burst open. Daemon stepped out, shotgun in hand. He took aim at the pickup where the woman had disappeared behind, having a clear view of that side of the vehicle.

Baldie was screaming as he rolled around and padded the blood-soaked area of where his dick and balls had been. Long-beard was groaning but laying still.

Bobby hopped down and over to Baldie. The man was shitting himself, the brown sludge pouring out of the cavernous hole like a slowly squeezed bottle of brown and red-colored salad dressing. The grass was smeared with the mess.

Daemon was telling whoever he was pointing his gun at to toss their gun away. A moment later, a handgun flew onto the porch from behind the pickup. "Now move it," Daemon said, and Cowboy and Bikini Top came out and stood in front of the vehicle's grill, hands up.

Jade came out from behind the pickup, a crossbow in her hands. Bobby guessed she'd found it inside the house and then snuck out one of the back windows so she could sneak up behind the enemy.

With the scene secure, Bobby racked his weapon, pointed it at No-crotch's head and disintegrated it with a pull of the trigger.

"You're fucking dead," Bikini Top said. "You hear me? Dead."

Bobby could barely hear her with the way his ears were ringing, but hear her he did, and walked up to Long-beard where he jammed the end of the gun barrel into the man's mouth, breaking most of his teeth. He held it there and looked at the woman before pulling the trigger and blowing Long-beard's brains six inches into the ground.

To Bobby's surprise, the woman growled and took off running toward him. Her eyes screamed death and her fingers were curled into claws. He pulled the shotgun out of the man's head, the end of the barrel caked in charred grizzle, and readied another round into play. A chunk of burnt Long-beard came free and plopped to the ground. He couldn't believe the woman had signed her death warrant so swiftly. She had to know he would kill her.

"Get back here, Mulva," Cowboy said.

Jade raised her crossbow.

Bobby raised his gun and hesitated. A moment later, an arrow flew from Jade's new toy and struck Bikini Top, a.k.a. Mulva, in the back of her head. Jade's uncle had taken Jade hunting—both bow and firearm—from the young age of nine until she turned fifteen when he got too drunk and sent a bullet into his belly that lodged against his spine, putting him in a wheelchair for life. Her aim with either type of weapon was incredible. The tri-tipped arrowhead protruded through Mulva's left eye socket, the eyeball popping out and onto the ground. Her angry expression faltered into one of deadpan as her legs gave out and she collapsed face-first.

To Bobby's surprise, Cowboy remained calm.

Jade laughed as she loaded another arrow.

"Well, that went well," Daemon said.

Cowboy's chest rose and fell as he took an obviously deep breath, then said, "What do you all want?"

"Not to upset over your friends?" Daemon asked.

"Hired and replaceable help."

"The woman, too?" Jade asked.

"Plenty more where she came from. Now get on with it and tell me what you want. I'm a businessman."

"Guns," Daemon said. "We want guns."

"You could've just asked," Cowboy said, shaking his head. "I've got guns. Lots of guns. But we've gotten off to such a bad start that I might have to charge you extra."

Jade pointed her crossbow at the man.

"Kill me and you get nothing."

"Oh, we ain't going to kill you," Jade said and fired an arrow into the man's thigh.

"Argh," he groaned and fell to one knee. "Bitch."

"But we can make it more or less painful for you to tell us," Jade finished.

Cowboy stood, wincing. "I ain't telling you shit." He pushed the arrow in further, then grabbed the head and pulled it out of his leg. Blood leaked from the wound, darkening the pant leg.

"Wow, you're like a superhero or something," Jade said.

"You made your point," Cowboy said. "But how do I know you won't kill me after I take you to the weapons?"

Jade rolled her eyes. "You don't. Duh."

Bobby picked up the gun Long-beard had dropped. It was a Smith and Wesson 1911 style .45. It felt heavy. He popped out the magazine, saw that it was indeed loaded and then shoved the mag back into place. Pulling back the slide, sunlight glinted off the brass casing of a bullet in waiting.

Surveying the situation, he made an executive decision, walked up behind Cowboy as Jade was threatening to pin the man's penis to his asshole if he didn't take them to the guns, and shot the man in the back of his head. Brain and skull decorated the porch steps and Daemon's shoes.

"What the hell, Bobby?" Daemon asked.

Jade laughed.

"You wanted guns," Bobby said, motioning to his own .45. "Got one here, you got one there, and we got two shotguns. I'd say we're good. We can't hang around here any longer. We got to go."

"Not cool, man," Daemon said, slipping the gun formerly held by Cowboy into his pants. "We could've used more weapons and then had some fun with him. Hunted him or something."

"We got what we came for and then some. Got to kill more than we planned. Scratch an itch early. Now it's time to go."

Daemon nodded. "You're right. That's why I keep you around—to keep me in check."

The bodies in the yard were left where they fell. Two cans of kerosene were found in the shed in the backyard. The bodies were doused and burned, along with the house. It was Bobby's idea to make the scene resemble Brewmeyer's. Let the cops come up with a reason, drugs or something. Only the arrows Jade fired were collected, cleaned off, and would be reused.

Once the house was lit up, they left, knowing the smoke would eventually lead to someone calling the fire department.

Chapter Twenty

Despite the few weeks that had passed, Amber still was not right. A good night's sleep was impossible. If she wasn't tossing and turning, she was waking sweat-lined and startled from one kind of nightmare or another. Her bed had become like a pit of despair. Her rape and all that accompanied it came to life when she laid her head down. She'd been doing a good job of hiding her emotional ups and downs. Putting up a front—her happy face—had become a regular occurrence, and while she was getting good at it she was also getting tired of it. Crying helped, but it was temporary. There was no one to talk to. She was embarrassed and didn't want her friends looking at her differently, as a victim or someone damaged.

Most of her time was spent alone or with her brother, Jason. He wasn't like most kids his age. For him, she especially made sure to act like nothing was wrong when what she really wanted to do was to curl up and die. She took him bowling, to the movies, for walks and bike rides, even though her mind was usually elsewhere. Often, she would zone out on the past, on Rex and the others, then return to the present when her brother asked her if she'd heard what he'd said. She'd smile, nod and fake that she had or simply ask him to repeat it.

Whether subtle or not, she knew the kid picked up on her true moods and states of mind. He'd always been great at seeing people's ticks and tells. Seeing through her façade was no different. He knew something was wrong, but didn't pester her. Said he would always be there for her. "Sometimes just having someone to talk with helps, even someone like me who might not be the best someone, but at least it would be someone that loves you." That had made her cry and she'd nearly squeezed him to death.

She'd come close to telling him the truth, or at least something close to it, the words always on the tip of her tongue. But ultimately, she'd decided against it. The kid was having a hard enough time in school and she didn't want to burden a twelve-year-old with serious adult issues.

Jason did well with his studies. He had skipped two grades, but in doing so he was always around older kids. Even when he had been among peers his own age he had trouble fitting in. *Picked on* had become synonymous with Jason.

So all in all, she would not involve him.

Sleep. She wanted a good night of it. Sleeping pills and other drugs were out of the question. Besides being somewhat nervous about taking such things, she wasn't going to rely on them and then wind up dependant on them. Smoke a little pot? Yes, she had, and it helped her fall asleep, but it did nothing to quell her nightmares of Rex or the security guard or the sorority sisters from raping her. In her dreams, they all had.

She didn't understand why she had dreams of each person violating her. Why not just Rex? Why so many different individuals? In each dream, she was always held down by people she despised—sorority sisters, campus security, multiple copies of Rex as if he were the product of cloning—and violated with fists, corn on the cob, knives, pledge paddles and once with Rex's penis, the large thing hissing at her before it entered her.

Sleep mostly came in half-hour increments and afternoon naps. Irritability followed her like a shadow. Lately, it had gotten to the point where her patience was virtually non-existent. She barked at her parents, co-workers and even customers which left her on the last warning from her boss.

One morning she'd snapped at Jason when he spilled his orange juice at the kitchen table and soaked her pants.

"What the hell, you little shit," she'd scolded. Her anger wouldn't stop and she felt like it was filling her. No way to shut it off. She wanted to hurt someone, hurt him. "You stupid little shithead. With all those smarts and you can't even pick up a glass without spilling it, you clumsy moron."

Jason stared at her, mouth agape.

"What?! What the hell are you looking at? Get something to clean this mess up with."

She stormed out of the kitchen and up to her room. While there, she caught a glimpse of her reflection in the mirror and barely recognized herself. Bags in duplicate took up space below her eyes. Her flesh was not just pale, but splotchy pale. Pimples decorated her forehead and chin.

Then as if she'd been whacked upside her head with a caning stick, her anger dissipated as quickly as it had arrived. Rex was still violating her. Still had a hold on her and was tearing her apart little by little. If she didn't get her emotions under control, she'd be changed for the worse forever. Would become a different, miserable person.

Knowing the old Amber was dead, she also knew that a more normal and happy Amber could become a reality again. People returned back from terrible events. To do so meant the violator hadn't completely won. The rape was a won battle, but the war was lost because she would come back from the damage he had caused. It would take hard work, even therapy, but she was sure she could do it.

She returned to the kitchen and discovered the spilled orange juice had been cleaned up. Jason's pancakes and eggs remained uneaten and he was nowhere to be found. After calling his name, she checked the living room, den, his bedroom and finally his laboratory—as he liked to call it—in the basement, the place where he ran experiments and built things like his drone. He was sitting on one of the workbench stools with his head down and arms wrapped around his legs that were tucked to his chest. She heard him sniffling.

Her heart felt like it dropped into her stomach.

"Hey kiddo," she said and walked up behind him. He flinched and wiped at his face. For as brilliant as he was, he was still just a twelve-year-old boy. "I'm sorry for speaking to you like I did."

"Okay." He remained in his curled up position.

Amber felt her anger rising again. She was so pissed at herself and whacked the side of her head using her hand. If she could kick her own ass she would. Then realizing how she was losing control, she inhaled and exhaled a few times and let her anger go. She hugged Jason from behind, pressing her cheek against his and again saying how sorry she was.

"I've got no excuse," she said. "I know spilling your juice was an accident. Perfectly normal. It happens to the best of us. Hell, I've done worse. Do you forgive me?"

He nodded and continued to wipe away tears. She let go of him and spun him around so he faced her. "I've been working too much and letting things from my past get to me. I'm not going to allow those things to affect me anymore. I'm going to make changes. Maybe even talk to someone. A professional."

"You can talk to me," he said.

"If I felt I could, I would. You know that."

"I've known something was wrong from the minute you came home from college. Something awful must have happened to you while you were there. It could be any number of things. I won't guess and try to read your facial expressions and tells, and I won't beat myself up trying to figure it out. No point worrying if I don't know what it is."

She stared at him, admiring how brilliant and adult-like he was, then said, "I'll tell you this: something bad did happen. I was hurt, but I wasn't destroyed. Wounds take time to heal, and when I do fully heal I'll be stronger than before. Trust me, I'm going to be okay."

"I do trust you," he said and hugged her.

After a few moments, they separated. "I have to get to work, but are you going to be okay now?"

"Yup." He vehemently nodded.

She rubbed his head and laughed, feeling warm inside for the first time in weeks. "See you tonight," she said and hurried out of the basement and off to work.

Amber arrived home to a sobering scene. Her brother's drone lay in pieces on the kitchen table. It appeared to have been crushed, the plastic flattened and jagged. Her mother was at the sink washing off vegetables for dinner.

"What happened?" Amber asked.

"Some little bastards . . . that's what happened," Judy said not turning around.

"Someone did this?"

"He went to the park with his drone," she said, placed a red pepper in a bowl off to the side, shut off the faucet and faced Amber. "Some bullies from school were there. Older kids. First, they stole the remote controller, then flew the thing into the side of a building. It crashed from there and then they stomped on it while holding him in a bear hug. He managed to kick one of the kids in the balls, but that only pissed them off. They punched him in his stomach and gave him a black eye. Besides the physical stuff, which is bad enough, they verbally assaulted him to no end. I could barely understand him he was so upset."

Amber couldn't move. Her fingers burned from her clenched fists. She focused on the broken drone, the thing a representative of how her brother was feeling. Her mother kept speaking but the woman's words were nothing more than meaningless muffled nonsense. Amber's peripheral vision was fading as her focus intensified.

You need to do something about this, The Voice screamed. *You're a victim. A coward who did nothing. Who took what she was given and accepted it. You want that for Jason? It'll only get worse for him, you know? Bullies need to be taught a lesson. Need to be stopped. They need to know if you fuck with Jason, you fuck with the devil.*

"Amber?" her mother said loudly, pulling Amber back to reality.

Amber's face was warm and felt like it might burst. She sucked in a breath and let it out. *Trying to kill yourself? Have to remember to breathe, woman.*

"What's wrong, your face . . ?"

"I'm fine, just pissed."

You haven't even asked how Jason's doing. If he's up in his room or in the basement. Don't you care?

"Shut up, of course I care," she said aloud.

"Excuse me?" her mother said, the woman's eyebrows sky-rocketing up her forehead.

"Nothing. How's Jason?"

"He's upset. Shaken. How do you think he'd be?"

"Where is he?"

"In his room. If he's sleeping, leave him be."

Amber left the kitchen and went upstairs. She stood outside his door and stared at the Do Not Enter Unless You Want To sign and almost laughed despite how angry she was feeling. She held her stomach when the giggles came on. Her anger grew as the laughing commenced, the act uncontrollable. It didn't make sense. Raising her right hand, she smacked herself. Once. Twice. The sting was real and acted like a switch, shutting off whatever it was that caused her to—

Crack up. That's what happening. You're losing it.

Amber turned the knob and entered the room. Jason lay on his bed staring at the ceiling. The flesh around his left eye was plum-colored. A chill swept through her, causing the hairs on her arms to stand. She approached the bed and sat next to him. "How are you feeling?"

"Sad," he said flatly.

A simple response that said so much. One word that spoke volumes and told a complete tale of his life at and after school. The way she had treated him that morning made her feel worse. He was such a loving and caring boy who deserved so much better.

"I know kids can be jerks," she said. "They aren't happy with themselves, or they're jealous. Bullies are results of that kind of crap."

"I know. I've done plenty of research on bullies. Figured it was the best thing to do in my situation. But the truth is they never want to be like me. They like being normal and believing people look up to them or are afraid of them. I like being me. I'm not better than they are, but I am more intelligent. I don't fit in. I'm fine with me being me, but they aren't. They are a constant reminder of how different I am."

Amber's stomach tightened.

"How long have they been bothering you?"

"Those particular ones—for the last year. But in general, I've been picked on all my life, and I'm only twelve. But it was never like this. Those guys don't let up. Whenever they see me they call me names. Poke, push and punch me." His voice cracked. "Things aren't getting easier. Life is getting harder." He turned away and Amber heard him crying.

She rubbed his back softly and wanted to tell him things would be okay, but the words wouldn't come. Because they were a lie. High school was tough on a lot of students. But the real world was tougher. It was a place where decisions were made and people did things that counted and were more detrimental. To tell him life was going to get better was rubbish.

"Look, the world isn't fair. Nothing says it's supposed to be, but then again, nothing says it shouldn't be. It's how you make it. It isn't your fault that you're smarter than your peers. There is no easy answer. The solution is to involve your teachers, talk with mom and dad, me, and do what you have to do in order to make it through. You need to use what happens to you, take whatever you can from it, learn and let it make you stronger. I'd love to tell you things get easier after high school, but they don't. The world is full of assholes."

Her thoughts went to Rex and what he'd done to her.

That's right. He'll always be with you. Inside you. Forever and ever.

Amber put her hands to the sides of her head. "Shut up. Leave me alone."

Jason turned toward her with a perplexed look on her face. "What?"

Amber lowered her hands. "I . . . I was just showing you something. A technique among many. Sometimes you need to get mad and let it out. Scream, shout, punch something. Whatever works."

Jason smiled and sat up. "Really?"

She was relieved he bought her lie and that it could even possibly help him. "See how I shocked you into another state of mind?"

"And people think I'm weird."

"You're not weird. You're special. As special as they come, and don't you ever forget that." Something clicked inside her and she wanted to cry. Clearing her throat, she fought off the emotion. "Bullies and scumbags, like those kids, will grow up to be bigger assholes and scumbags. Ignore and stay away from them as much as you can."

"I try, but they seek me out. When they see me down the hall, they call me names. It's like I have a bully-attracting disease. They won't leave me alone. I went to one of my teachers and all that did was put a bigger target on my back."

"Bullies are a part of life," she said softly. "It's good to learn about them now. Get it over with. Figure them out. I know you'll do it. We'll get through this together."

"Thanks, Amber," Jason said.

"Anytime." She turned and left his room, shutting the door behind her.

That's it. Spew the bullshit. Spray it all over the room.

Amber told herself she was going to ignore The Voice. She was going to get better and get rid of it. Ignoring it was the first step.

I'm here to stay, like Rex's stink. What you need to do is get the names of the kids who fucked with Jason and make them pay.

Amber understood that people talked to themselves. It was normal to do so. A person's inner voice was essential to survival. Essential to plain old boring life. It sifted through rights and wrongs. But the voice she heard was more than inner thoughts. She'd even given it a name. The Voice had been born or created by her rape. Or maybe it had been there the whole time and was set free by the horrendous experience. It was like the damaged part of her had separated itself and had a mind of its own. She'd had some sort of split.

It was her, all her, but unidentifiable and uncontrollable. She was afraid of it, but at the same time, she wanted to listen to it and gain strength from it. It was the dark part of her soul reaching out. It could allow her to do things she normally wouldn't do for one reason or another. As long as she respected it, got help with her issues, it wouldn't consume her, but would allow her to never again be a victim. It was ultimately a coping mechanism and she had to let it run its course.

Stop pondering shit, and listen. You can't let your brother suffer anymore. The defenseless like him, like how you used to be since I've come along, need to be defended.

What was she supposed to do, maim the bullies? Kill them? Is that what her darkness was telling her? She waited for an answer, for what her dark side wanted.

Teach them a lesson. You did nothing to those who wronged and hurt you. It's time to begin anew.

Amber told herself there was nothing she could have done without making things ugly for her.

Of course there were. Still are. Things you can do.

Amber asked if The Voice also meant for her to kill Rex. Or to cut off his cock? Or hurt the others who didn't help her? Scar or mutilate them? Punish all those who didn't help her?

Yes. Yes. Yes. Once a rapist, always a rapist. He doesn't deserve to have a penis.

The truth was that she'd love to slice off his balls. But thinking something was far removed from actually doing it. Thoughts were just that and free to roam around her mind. What she needed to do was concentrate on helping her brother.

You're pathetic! Getting raped made you weak!

Amber screamed FUCK YOU inside her head. She also understood she needed to do something to those bullies, despite their age. What were they, thirteen? Fourteen? Fifteen max? It didn't matter.

I know what you're thinking. Play it safe, right? Tell their parents. Sure, do that. MORON. Who do you think they learned their bullying ways from? They'll have no sympathy for Jason, and when they find out a girl is fighting a boy's battle, they'll really want Jason to suffer. REAL SMART, AMBER.

What the hell was she supposed to do? How could she help him? Then it dawned on her, a wicked, yet not too evil, way to exact vengeance.

In her room, she went into her closet and rifled around the top shelf until she found the blanket she was looking for. Taking it down, she unwrapped the BB gun, a CO2 powered toy—*toy? It's a fucking gun. Don't be naive*—and admired it. Next to the stock were two CO2 cartridges and a box of BBs.

Her father had wanted to teach her about guns and how to shoot them. She wanted no part of it. In a strange compromise, her father bought her a BB gun and together they practiced shooting with it. He'd said it would be a great squirrel deterrent, but there was no way she was killing an animal with that thing. Her father had thought after practicing with the BB gun—and getting good at hitting targets—that she'd want to move up to rifles. But she hadn't wanted to.

Guns were loud, obnoxious and only good for killing people or hunting for survival. And while she understood they were essential in the right hands and that hunting was fine, she had no interest. She kept the BB gun, occasionally taking it out to fire at cans and bottles, but eventually stowed it away where it sat in her closet wrapped in a blanket.

She hadn't understood her dad's desire to have her become a gun enthusiast, but guessed it was because her grandfather had been one, and there was no way Jason would be one, so she had been his only hope on passing along his knowledge and something he enjoyed.

This is good. Really good.

Yes, Amber did feel good about what she was going to do.

Chapter Twenty-one

Three days passed since the events at Dirk's. The fire department had been alerted to the billowing smoke rising into the air like smoldering volcano ready to erupt. Soon after the first tanker arrived, the police were called. The crime scene was immediately linked to the events at Brewmeyers. With their crimes associated elsewhere, the trio in the clear, they decided it was time to start the new game.

The Camry, including the plastic hubcaps, was coated in maroon-colored Plasti-Dip. An axe, baseball bat, machete, crossbow and a morning star—the medieval spiked-ball-and-chain having been purchased online years ago by Bobby as a decoration to go along with his many daggers and swords. Bobby had been a huge Dungeons and Dragons fan and loved collecting weaponry that represented the fantasy age.

Before heading out, the trio flipped a coin to see who would get to play first. Jade won and took up position in the Camry's passenger seat. The fake license plate was clicked into position and the scanner was tuned to the proper frequency before Daemon drove off Bobby's property.

Bobby sat in the back and was in charge of handing weapons to the player as well as keeping an extra eye on the surrounding area. They headed to the eastern part of the county to an area where the houses were separated by acres of lush forest, keeping views from windows and people in their yards off the witness list.

They drove for thirty minutes before coming upon a tall man with salt and pepper hair jogging alongside the road, heading in the same direction as the Camry. Daemon slowed the car.

"Motherfucker's all mine," Jade said. Her chest felt like it swelled as her pulse sped up. Her limbs tingled with excitement. She donned the hockey mask and reached back for the crossbow, the weapon a little bulky when it came to maneuvering in the car. Daemon was conked on his head.

"Fuck, babe," he said and rubbed his noggin.

"Stop whining," Jade said, stuck her foot in the weapon's stirrup, pulled back the string until it locked into place and then loaded the arrow. She climbed halfway out of the window, taking the crossbow with her. Fighting the wind, she aimed the weapon. The car drew closer to the prey. Despite having him in her sights, she waited.

The Camry drew closer.

She waited.

At any time she could've put an arrow anywhere on the jogger she wanted. At least she thought so. Shooting from a moving vehicle at a moving target could prove tougher than she imagined. It was a new test. One she was looking forward to. But she also wanted her first victim to know he was going to die.

Closer.

Closer.

She thought she could smell the man, a slight hint of cologne and body odor. Bobby was asking what she was waiting for, and it pissed her off. This was her time and she didn't want to be bothered. "Don't puss out now," he said and Jade thought about turning the weapon on him and making him her first.

Concentration back on the jogger, she moved her aim from ass to back to neck and head. She couldn't decide. A kill shot would mean the man had no idea what happened. No fear. No waiting for death to come, knowing there was nothing he could do to save himself. She could shoot him in the calf. He'd go down, be unaware and it would take him time to realize what had happened. He could get away because there was no getting out of the car. That was one of the rules.

Fuck the rules. If it came to her having to leave the car, she'd do it. Forfeit her points. All she cared about was the kill. But it wouldn't come to that. No. She now knew how she had to do it.

"Hey asshole," she yelled.

The jogger glanced over his shoulder. His eye grew wide, his face transforming into a mask of terror. Jade pulled the trigger and sent arrow flying. The projectile pierced his cheek and tore right through it, disappearing into the foliage ahead. He stumbled forward and crashed face-first to the asphalt. His legs came up over his head, his back arching like a horseshoe, before they whipped back down.

Daemon stopped the car a few feet ahead of the jogger. Jade loaded another arrow as the man lay on the road barely moving. A pool of blood formed around his head. She took aim, waiting. He placed his hands on the road and pushed his upper body off the ground. Blood rained down from his mashed nose and mouth, the orifice gaping. His jaw had been shattered and hung low. He looked at Jade and she saw the fear and disbelief in his eyes. She nodded and fired another arrow. It sank into the man's forehead, jerking it back before all the life left him and his body fell limp. She hollered in triumph.

Daemon hit the gas and took off.

Jade slid back into the car and handed Bobby her weapon and hockey mask. "That was fucking awesome," she said, feeling as if she'd orgasmed ten times.

"Nice kill, but you needed two shots to finish him," Bobby said.

"I wanted it that way moron," Jade spat. "Wanted him to know he was going to die and see that I was the one who was going to end his ass.

"Damn, babe," Daemon said. "You're one evil woman."

"Thank you, darling," she said and planted a kiss on his cheek while she rubbed his crotch. "I could fuck the hell out of you right now."

"Unless I'm allowed to watch and whack my meat, you two lovebirds can wait. Daemon's up next and then it's my turn."

"I'd love an audience," Jade said as she sat back in her seat.

"Oh, you'd consider it would you?" Bobby asked.

"Hell yeah, but not with you watching, perv," Jade said.

They drove to the opposite side of the town limits, making sure to avoid the busiest roads and going nowhere near the actual town. Bobby was constantly reminding Jade not to speed, the woman a demon behind the wheel. The scanner made getting pulled over virtually impossible, but there was always the chance a cop could be sitting somewhere and hadn't reported his position. There could also be the chance they got into an accident, and having a car full of weapons would surely garner attention.

"Stop worrying so much, man," Jade said as the tires screeched around a corner.

"If I don't who the hell will?" Bobby asked.

"Shit, up ahead," Daemon said, pointing at the elderly man walking to his mailbox.

"Babe, you're finally going to pop your cherry," Jade said and rubbed his thigh.

The man stood in front of the mailbox and pulled the door open.

Most of the houses along the road were set back and had driveways that disappeared behind lush forest, making the area a perfect hunting ground.

Daemon pulled on the hockey mask and leather gloves. He had Bobby hand him the sledgehammer. The smashing tool's handle had been cut down to make it more manageable during their game.

The Camry drew closer to his target.

Daemon climbed halfway out the window, using the seatbelt to keep him supported in the event he should fall out. He brought the sledgehammer out next. The wind made it feel like he was dragging it through water.

The man had his arm inside the mailbox.

The car drew nearer and Daemon felt his pulse quicken.

The man pulled out pieces of mail, then bent his legs and peered into the box, making sure he hadn't missed anything.

Using both arms, Daemon raised the sledgehammer.

The man closed the mailbox lid and was busy glancing through his mail.

Daemon was amazed how people took their safety for granted. Joggers, bikers and everyone else who walked along the road put their lives in driver's hands. What did people really know about their fellow drivers, those neighbors they knew so well? Small town security and neighborly politeness was bullshit. There were plenty of crazy and drunk drivers. Old people who could barely see and young kids who cared more how they appeared in a car and what music cranked out the speakers or if they dropped their phone and took their eyes off the road to pick it up or read a text or the hundred other distractions that led to death. A vehicle was a death machine in waiting, and how a man could stand on a part of the road and not even look at who was approaching was beyond Daemon—one of the least give-a-shit people in the world.

Daemon was on him now.

The man looked up as the sledgehammer sailed toward him, his expression of surprise priceless. Jade was right in wanting to see the prey's final state of being.

Preparing for impact like a Major League baseball player preparing to hit a homerun, Daemon squeezed the handle as the hammer smashed into the man's head. The man's nose vanished first, crumbling the glasses that had been hanging on the end of his bulbous nose. His head caved in like a freshly baked cherry pie and then exploded in blood and gore. The hammer-head caught in the man's skull and was yanked out of Daemon's hands. The corpse's legs were taken out from under, and then it crashed back down to the asphalt, mail scattered around the body like memories knocked free.

"Stop the car, I lost the sledgehammer," Daemon said.

Jade hit the breaks.

"No leave it," Bobby said. "We can't ever risk going back to a crime scene. The tool has no prints on it."

Jade looked at Daemon who had crawled back onto his chair.

"You heard the man. Go," he said. "We ain't paying him for his looks."

Jade laughed and sped off. "Damn, this shit is so much fucking fun."

CHAPTER TWENTY-TWO

AMBER WAS RELIEVED SHE hadn't hurt those kids. She could have. Easily. Sitting just inside the tree line that ran alongside the park, she'd sighted the biggest of the bullies, but ultimately held off shooting the kid. The weapon was only a BB gun. Wearing camouflage pants and shirt, dark green, black and brown face paint, she would never be seen. She could have definitely gotten off a few shots before the bastards figured out what was going on and took off running. Then she'd make sure they got her typed letter telling them if they bullied anyone again, next time the BBs would be bullets. According to Jason, the bullies picked on other students too, but seemed to focus their hate mostly on him. In order not to have any blowback on her or Jason, the letter would have had to be about bullying in general.

The latest episodes of violence around her town had been the reason she changed her mind. People had been killed in gruesome fashion and there seemed to be no reason for it, as if a reason would have made the killings more understandable. The victims had been shot with arrows and bludgeoned to death. Reading about them in the local paper had turned her stomach and she lost her need for violence. And these deaths were after hearing about Mr. Brewmeyer's murder and the murder of a local drug dealer. Then yesterday there had been more attacks.

A woman walking along the road had been beheaded. Another person out for a stroll had been set on fire and now lay dying in the hospital with no chance of survival. Then there was a jogger who'd had her left arm sliced off just below the shoulder. She'd said she looked back just in time to see someone hanging out of a car wearing a hockey mask and swinging a machete. The attack was coming at her head. She managed to dodge out of the way and keep her head intact, but the jungle-clearing tool went right through her arm, severing it completely. She then tumbled into the woods and the car sped away.

Amber wondered what the hell was going on. Small towns weren't supposed to have maimings and killing sprees. At worst, bar brawls and drunk drivers. The cops had no clue if the house-burning murders and spree-killings were related. But they did believe it was possible that the people being killed alongside roads was the result of some sick cult moving through the area. The local police chief had called in the State Troopers for extra patrols.

As much as Amber wanted the killers to move on, she would rather have them stay in town and get caught. It didn't seem right to celebrate another town receiving them. It was selfish to simply want them gone and not captured or killed.

If there was a plus to everything going on it was that The Voice was almost gone. It only reared its ugly head on occasion—like when she was overly stressed to the point of steaming rage. The last time she'd heard it was after some asshole customer kept grabbing her ass whenever she walked by. She'd told him to cut it out, but he was drunk and wouldn't listen. Laughed about it with his friends. Then he'd left a penny for a tip and complained to the manager that she had done a terrible job and was rude.

The next time he came in The Voice demanded that she poison his drink. She ignored it, not wanting to do anything so extreme. Instead, she borrowed the cook's Visine eye drops—the man a habitual pot smoker—and laced the customer's beer, quickly sending him to the bathroom where she heard him heaving his guts out. The Voice called her a pussy, but she felt good about her decision. She would continue to dose the guy's food and drink—whether he was her customer or not—until he stopped coming in.

That had been the last time she'd heard The Voice. The longer she ignored it, the more it died.

Chapter Twenty-three

With so many cops in the area, the trio of killers had to slow down. It had been a few days since their last outing, and that hadn't been a kill. Jade was still fuming over only severing the arm of a female jogger.

They hung around Bobby's house, getting wasted and shooting their guns at birds, squirrels and bottles. Compared to what they had been doing, their time now was beyond boring.

"I'm going to the Big M," Jade said. "You guys want anything?"

"Beer and smokes," Daemon said.

"Chips, all kinds," Bobby said.

Jade drove Bobby's Shelby to town. She took an out of the way route, enjoying the fresh air and music blasting from the speakers. She hadn't seen a single person out and about save for passing cars. People were scared. The police had urged residents to stay in groups and indoors until the perps were apprehended. When walking along the road, they were told to pay attention to approaching vehicles and move way off to the side. Killing would be getting more and more difficult.

They had only killed a small number of people and the town was in a panic. Jade had hoped to be able to kill for a while and was surprised with the rapid increase in police presence. Laying low would be tough, but it was something they had to do for the foreseeable future. Let the town relax a little, get the troopers out, and then they could kill again. Maybe they would even move on to killing in another town. She would have to wait and see. Getting high, really high, seemed to take the edge off of the need to kill. The damn game was fun, but she imagined they'd find other ways to kill. Killing was what mattered. Powerful. The ability to end someone, to see their fear, was the best drug she'd ever consumed.

Jade parked the Shelby in the Big M's lot and went inside. She grabbed a shopping cart, making sure none of the wheels were out of whack, and went aisle to aisle loading in goodies. The last aisle was where the refrigerated beverages were located, including the beer. She stacked a few cases into the cart and was heading down the aisle, passed the corridor that led to the restrooms, when she was yanked from behind into the dark hallway and into the arms of a bear-like man with a python grip.

"Heya, girlie," he said, and before she could scream, he clamped a meaty paw over her mouth.

Jade kicked and struggled to break free, her arms pinned to her sides by a single one of his, making her efforts were fruitless.

"Now, now. Stop your fussing or I'll snap your neck and be done with you."

Jade remembered where she was—in a supermarket— and relaxed. The worst the guy could do was hurt her, stab her, maybe even kill her, but he wouldn't be able to rape her. If anything, it was close to closing time and a sweeper or someone telling her it was time to head to checkout would come along. If he pulled her into one of the restrooms, she'd be in trouble. She wondered why he hadn't already done so and guessed they were locked.

"Are you going to behave?" he asked.

She nodded and realized the air had a cherry-scented cigar odor to it.

"If you scream, you die."

He removed his hand and Jade felt the sweat from his palms clinging to the flesh around her mouth. Still held in a bear hug, she couldn't wipe it away and shivered with repulsion.

His voice . . . Cherry-scented cigars . . . There was something familiar about those things.

And then she knew. It was Bud Kyle. The fat prick had been friends with Daemon until the night he hit on Jade behind Daemon's back, and when she'd told him to fuck off, he'd tried to force himself on her. She'd fought him off, but took a few smacks and wound up with a bloody lip and a black eye. Bud had gone into hiding after that, avoiding his usual hangout spots, until one night when Daemon beat the shit out of him as he was coming out of his mom's house.

"What the fuck, Bud?" Jade said.

"Tell me something, Jade, is that pussy hair of yours purple too? Or are you bald down there?"

Before she could tell him to fuck off he covered her mouth again and pulled her close, her back pressed against his chest. Holding her tightly with one arm, he slithered his other hand down her belly and into her jean shorts, then under her panties. His fingers found her hole and he plunged two inside, the thick digits like cold and bloated worms.

She kicked his shins and dug her nails into his forearms. He growled, spun around with her and slammed her against the wall, pressing his weight on her. His grip remained strong and his two fingers went deeper.

Disgust, worse than thousands of cockroaches crawling into her pussy, ran through her and she wanted to vomit. Her skin rippled with goose bumps. He was laughing, enjoying it all.

A moment later, Jade let it all go and relaxed her body, sagging in his grip. She wasn't going to give the scumbag the satisfaction he wanted. Not all of it anyway. He continued to pump his fingers into her and asked her if she liked it. Finally, he withdrew his hand from her pants and held them up to his nose. "You smell delicious," he said, then stuck the fingers into his mouth and sucked her juices off them.

"I told you I'd get you bitch," he said. He spun her around so she faced him. Could smell his cigar breath and her pussy-juice on it. Furious, she kneed him in the balls, but it did little to hurt him. "Little cunt." He threw her against the opposite wall where her head smacked the cinderblock. Stars bloomed across her vision for a moment. His hand closed around her throat.

Pinned to the wall, he lifted her off the floor. "Tell anyone about this, and I'll kill you and that shitfuck of a boyfriend of yours," he said and launched a fist into her gut. The air was expelled from her lungs. Pain radiated to her spine and kidneys. "You're lucky I found you here, cunt. If it had been someplace quieter, I'd have fucked you into a coma."

Jade was released. She fell to her feet, but her legs gave out and she crumbled to the floor. Waiting for another blow of some kind, she laughed. And laughed. And laughed.

When nothing happened, she looked up and saw that Bud had left. Hurting, she got to her feet, rage seeping from her pores like sweat from a bodybuilder. The cherry odor still hung in the air, making her sick.

Her first reaction was to run to her car, grab her tire iron and beat the shit out of Bud before he could drive away. Instead, she went to her cart, grabbed one of the Labatt bottles and downed its contents, then smashed the bottle on the floor. "Clean up in aisle ten," she said and broke into uncontrollable laughter, only stopping when an idea popped into her head.

A deliciously, wicked idea.

Chapter Twenty-four

"I'M GOING TO KILL him," Daemon said and sprang out of the recliner he was sitting on.

"Wait," Jade said, laying her hands on him as he brushed past her.

"Don't try and stop me, babe."

"Bobby," she called out. "I need your help."

Daemon flew through the house, passing by the kitchen where Bobby was eating ice-cream and reading a comic book. Jade was right behind Daemon, catching the front door before it closed on her.

"What's going on?" Bobby asked.

"Get out here and help me before he does something that gets him tossed in prison."

Bobby sprinted outside and raced over to the Camry just ahead of a storming Daemon.

"Get out of my way, Bobby," Daemon said.

Holding his hands out, Bobby asked what happened.

"Bud, Kyle attacked Jade. Stuck his fat fingers in her. He needs to die."

Bobby's mouth hung open.

Jade knelt by the Camry's rear tire and held a knife to it.

Daemon grabbed Bobby by his arms and tossed him aside, then reached for the door handle when Jade said, "Not another step, babe, or I'll pop this tire and the rest."

Daemon glared at her. "Get away from the car."

"Dude, when did this happen?" Bobby asked.

Daemon ignored him and stepped toward Jade.

"One more inch and the tire goes," Jade said. "I'll slash them all, Daemon. You know I will."

Daemon's chest rose and fell. His hands were fists at his sides. "Fuuuuuuc-ccckkkkkk," he yelled and slammed his fist on the car's roof.

"Babe, I know you're pissed," Jade said. "I fucking am too. If I'd wanted to, I could've gutted that pig at the market. But we need to be smart about stuff now."

Bobby's eyebrows arched.

"Guess you're rubbing off on me," Jade said.

Daemon threw up his arms. "So what, forget about him? Let the mother-fucker walk away?"

Jade stood, folded the knife, and slipped it into her pocket. "No, idiot. I'd sooner slice off my clit than let him get away with touching me." She shivered. "I have a plan. And it involves us fucking him up."

"No," Bobby said, stepping up and shaking his head. "We can't take any chances. Not now."

"I want to hear her plan," Daemon said.

Bobby rolled his eyes. "Let's hear it."

"Well . . ." Jade said. "I figured since we can't ride around and play The Game for a while, it doesn't mean we can't make home visits."

Chapter Twenty-five

After gathering their supplies, the trio piled into the Camry and headed over to Bud's neck of the woods. Daemon parked the car a mile up the road behind an abandoned bait and tackle shop. From there, they walked to Bud's place. At two in the morning, they wouldn't see much traffic, and if a vehicle did wind up coming along, they would simply hide in the tree line until it passed.

When they reached the property, they slid on their gloves and disguises, all of them wearing ski masks just to switch it up a bit. If caught on camera, the descriptions the cops had been given wouldn't match what they were currently wearing, further confusing the piggies.

Bud's front yard was mostly open grass with a few Oak trees, making the house clearly visible from the road. The nearest neighbor was three acres away, the house dark save for a small light coming from one of the windows.

Having been in Bud's house plenty of times when Daemon and Bud were friends, Daemon knew the layout. Bud had moved out when he turned eighteen, but after his mother passed away from a heart attack—his father having left when he was a baby—Bud moved back into the home. A paint-peeled, white wooden fence surrounded the sides and back of the yard, the thing in desperate need of a paint job.

The trio crept along the fence until they were in line with the house, then bolted to the attached one-car garage. From there, they went around back to the patio where the rear entrance was located. Daemon tried the door and found it unlocked. Bud hadn't changed a bit. The big oaf was like so many of the town's people. They felt safe. Locking a house up tight wasn't a priority. That might have been the way it was in the 50s and 60s, even the 90s, but in today's world, people needed to take heed of the dangerous individuals roaming the earth.

They slipped inside the house, the door leading to the kitchen. A cutout in the wall gave a view of the living room. The television was on, casting a dim glow around the room. Peering through the opening, Daemon saw two people sleeping on the couch, neither of them Bud. One was Gill Boumont. The other Tracy McMillan. Daemon knew them both. Losers to the core and good friends with Bud. They must've partied a little too hard and passed out. Beer cans littered the coffee table and floor.

Daemon looked at the others and held up two fingers, then pointed into the living room. Jade and Bobby nodded and followed him out of the kitchen. Bobby held a hunting knife with a serrated edge. Jade had her crossbow in hand. Daemon his machete, the .45 tucked in the waistband of his pants.

They stood in front of the slumbering pair. Daemon and Jade looked at Bobby and nodded, giving him the go ahead.

Bobby stepped up to the couch. The woman was resting alongside Gill. Her right arm and leg lay on top of him, her head nestled against his armpit. He put the tip of his knife to her temple and shoved it in, the blade disappearing easily. A trickle of blood leaked out of the incision. Her body jerked and then went still. Blood continued to run, turning her blonde hair red.

Bobby withdrew the knife from the corpse's head, then pressed the blood-slicked blade to the side of Gill's throat and sliced a gash across it. The initial cut wielded a few spurts of blood before it exited in waterfall-like fashion. The man awoke. He sat up and clutched at his throat, sending the dead woman to the floor. His mouth opened and it looked like he was trying to speak. Bobby backed away as the man got to his feet. He reached out and tripped over the corpse at his feet.

"He's making a bit too much noise, don't you think?" Daemon whispered.

Gill crawled forward leaving a river of crimson behind. Bobby stepped on the man's fingers with the heel of his boot and ground them into the carpet. The bones snapped and skin split. Gill's mouth opened, but no scream came forth.

Daemon understood Bobby's need to play with his prey, but they were there for Jade. The more time they wasted with Gill—who didn't have much left—the less Jade would have with Bud.

"Dude, kill him," Daemon said harshly.

"He's dead, just hasn't realized it yet."

"Enough of this shit," Jade said and shot an arrow into the man's head.

Bobby spun on her. "What the hell, Jade? He was mine!"

"Noise, moron. The asshole was making too much of it. Besides, I'm done wasting time here."

"I slit his throat so he wouldn't make any noise. I know what the fuck I'm doing."

"He's dead," Daemon said, stepping between them. "Time to move on. You got the kill, man. She only made it come quicker."

Bobby's jaw moved back and forth, the man clearly unhappy. "Fine. Let's do this."

After shutting off the television and allowing their eyes to adjust to the low level of light coming in through the windows, they made their way down the hall. They passed a bathroom that smelled like body odor, and then a room filled with garbage bags, a desk with a computer on it, and an exercise bike in the corner. At the end of the corridor were two doors, both slightly ajar. With gun in hand, Daemon checked the door on his right and found a bed, table and chairs, but no people. Turning his attention to the other door, he slowly pushed it open and slid into the room.

Bud lay naked on his back, his rotund belly like some giant, swelled blister ready to burst. Gentle snores filled the air. Next to him was a naked woman Daemon didn't recognize. Her feet hung a good foot off the bed, a bra hanging off her large toe. The air was heavy with the stench of sweat, semen and pussy. Daemon looked over his shoulder at Jade who was standing in the doorway and whispered, "You're up, babe."

She entered the room and smiled. Her and Daemon kissed for a moment, then with a flick from her forefinger, she turned the light switch position from off to on. The room exploded with bright light from the overhead bulbs.

"Ack, what the hell, Gill?" Bud moaned.

"Gill is a little dead right now and can't come out to play," Jade said.

Bud sat up quickly, coughing. The woman next to him didn't move, only complained about how bright the light was shining.

"What the—" Bud began, his voice groggy, but appearing fully awake now.

"You fucked with the wrong woman, Bud," Daemon said.

"So what, you here to rough me up a bit?"

"Not exactly," Jade said, then raised the crossbow and fired an arrow through the woman's ankle, the projectile stopping halfway though the leg. The woman bolted upright, screaming.

"Are you fucking crazy?" Bud shouted and reached for the nightstand where he yanked open the drawer.

Daemon kicked the drawer closed on Bud's hand, pinning it in place with his boot while his former friend howled in pain. He pressed the gun against Bud's greasy head and told him to slowly pull his hand out. Bud did so, then sat back and held his bruised hand to his chest. Daemon pulled a .38 Special out of the drawer and tossed it to Bobby.

Bud's female companion continued to wail.

"Bitch, shut the hell up or the next arrow goes through your skull," Jade said, having already loaded another projectile.

"You . . . You shot me. It fucking hurts." She continued to cry. "I'll never walk the same again."

Jade stood next to Daemon, handed him her crossbow and withdrew the machete from the sheath on his belt before returning to the woman. "I told you to shut the hell up." Jade tapped the machete against her palm.

The woman's cries turned to sobs and then she was quiet, but still shaking. "It hurts. Hurts so bad. I need to go to a hospital. I ain't part of whatever this is between you and Bud."

"Does your ankle hurt that badly?" Jade asked.

"Just let me go to a doctor," the woman whined as she held her leg.

"Why bother when I can get rid of the hurty part myself?" She raised the machete and swung fast, lopping off the foot, ankle and a few fingers due to the woman's inability to remove her hands in time. She screamed, her vocal cords like daggers against Daemon's ears. Blood gushed from the stump and spurted from the severed digits.

Jade shrugged. "Guess that didn't help much."

"Shut her up," Bobby said.

Jade thrust her arm forward and sent the machete's blade into the woman's mouth. She then jumped onto the bed and straddled the woman, forcing the steel down her throat. Gagging noises mixed with blood sounded. "Come on, slut, swallow my shit. Take it all in. Show daddy you can suck a good machete." The woman's arms flailed as she coughed and gagged, blood speckling Jade's face.

"What the fuck?" Bud said and attempted to hop off the bed when Daemon pistol-whipped him back onto it, creating a large and deep gash in his forehead.

When Daemon glanced back at Jade, she was holding up a dead woman. The corpse's head was arched back, lifeless eyes staring at the ceiling while the handle of the machete protruded out of her gaping mouth. Blood seeped from her neck where the blade had sliced through.

"She must have given great head," Jade said. She took a moment to admire her work, then focused on an unconscious Bud, his face caked in crimson from the wound on his forehead. "He better not be dead."

"Nope," Daemon said. "Just had to get him back into bed."

With effort, Jade pulled the machete out of the corpse's throat. The blade was caked in blood and pinkish esophageal flesh. She shoved the body away and it tumbled off the bed. "Come on, boys, time to strap this piggy down."

Bud was centered on the bed. Jade got the duct tape out of her bag and secured his wrists and ankles to the accompanying bedposts. "Looks good," she said, then sat on his stomach and slapped him awake.

As soon as his eyes opened, they focused on Jade. He blinked hard, then tried grabbing her. "What the hell?" He looked at his right wrist, then his left and sighed.

"Did you really think you would get away with violating me?"

"I was fucking stoned off my ass. I'm sorry. Okay. I hardly remember—"

Jade pressed the machete against his throat, silencing him. "Better like this." She drew a thin line of blood before stopping.

"Is Barb dead, I don't see her?" Bud asked.

"Was that the woman who swallowed my tool," she said, indicating the machete in hand.

"You're a sick bitch, you know that?"

"You really are stupid, aren't you?"

"You didn't have to kill her."

"Did she ever swallow your entire cock like she swallowed my machete?"

"Doesn't look like it would be difficult," Daemon said.

"Small dick alert," Jade said.

"Fuck you, guys," Bud said and spit in Jade's face.

Jade shook her head and said, "Tsk, tsk," then shoved the machete's blade between Bud's lips. "Now that wasn't very nice." She slowly moved the blade back and forth in saw-like fashion, giving Bud the ability to open his mouth farther than he ever thought possible. The big man cried out. "I could cut your fucking face in half if I wanted to." She withdrew the machete and sat up, resting the bloody tool at her side.

Tears streaked Bud's face as blood ran down his cheeks and into his mouth. "Please, there's got to be something we can do to work this out," he said, his speech slightly off. "I mean, I can pay you, or do something for you."

"You sure are stupid and funny," Jade said. "I'll be right back." She climbed off of him and left the room.

"Guys, please," Bud said, "you got to let me go. I'll do anything."

"Bud, if Jade hadn't stopped me, you'd have been dead much earlier," Daemon said.

"We were friends at one point, remember? I fucked up. I'll admit that."

"You more than fucked up, Bud. The first time was a fuck up. And I made sure you paid for that. This time you signed your death warrant."

Jade entered the room holding an electric carving knife. "Look what I found."

"Nice, babe."

"Now I can reenact some of my favorite scenes from one of my favorite movies—The Texas Chainsaw Massacre Part 2." She approached Bud while pressing the trigger on the knife, the serrated blade moving back and forth in a blur.

"Get away from me." Bud struggled, the tape on his wrists and ankles groaning, but holding firm.

Standing next to the bed, she told Daemon and Bobby to make sure Bud behaved during surgery. Bobby tossed Daemon his hunting knife. Daemon then held the tip of the blade against the corner of Bud's left eye socket. Bobby held the crossbow and asked if she wanted him to pin the man's leg to the mattress.

"Nah, I think he'll behave." Jade held onto Bud's thick thigh, brought the knife to life again with a press of the trigger before lowering it to his flesh. The steel easily cut into the meat. Bud screamed through clenched teeth, trying not to move. Jade guided the knife along, going from the top of his thigh to a few inches above the knee cap. Blood cascaded down the leg in rivulets, quickly soaking the sheet. Bud was trembling, tears streaming down his cheeks.

Jade forced her fingers under the skin, then peeled the flesh up and off. Bud howled in pain, quieting the wet, tacky sound of the flesh separating from the gelatinous muscle beneath. She held the slab of glistening skin out and admired her work. Bud's leg was a raw, exposed appendage ripe for infection. Jade poked the area repeatedly with her free hand, Bud adding yelps to his cries each time. "So soft," Jade said.

"Fuck you, bitch," Bud said, spittle flying from his lips. "Fuck you."

A pearl of blood rolled down his face from where the tip of Daemon's knife broke the skin next to his eye.

"I'm impressed, Bud," Jade said. "You hardly moved. I had a dog once that was like that when we took him to the vet. Was as still as a statue." She flung the skin over her shoulder, then picked up the knife and went to work on Bud's rib flesh, slicing down to the bone. Bud swore and cursed, Daemon's knife penetrating the eye-flesh and ball, turning the white pupil red.

Jade didn't stop there; she kept going, removing the skin from his knee caps next, then his other thigh, shins, forearms and nipples, piling it all neatly on the floor.

"Please . . . kill me," Bud drooled. He could barely lift his head.

"I should've brought my video camera, babe," Daemon said. "This would've been great to watch over and over again."

"No cameras," Bobby said, sitting in the chair, crossbow resting on his lap. "That's how assholes get caught."

"I think, with all this extraneous activity, I've made Bud tired. He needs energy." Jade picked up a slice of flesh. "Open his mouth."

Bud seemed to come to life again. "N . . . No."

Daemon held Bud's head and squeezed his mouth until it opened. Jade shoved in the skin, then Daemon pressed the man's jaw closed and covered his mouth. "Chew, piggy. Chew."

Bud screamed and bucked.

Jade got the electric knife blade under Bud's penis and across his ball sack. "Eat it or you lose them."

Bud was still. He stared at her, hate in his eyes. He began to chew, gagging every second until he lurched forward as far as his taped wrists would allow. Daemon lost his hold. Bud's mouth opened wide and the flesh was propelled forward by a stream of vomit that splashed over his belly.

"Gross," Jade said, jumping away from the bed.

"That's going to smell," Bobby said. "I feel like I'm part of some horror comedy from the 80s."

Breathing hard, Bud begged for them to stop. "Please, just let me go. I won't tell anyone it was you three."

Jade ran out of the room, quickly returning with a container of Kosher Salt in her hand.

"No," he said, shaking his head. "No. You can't. Please. I'm begging you. I'm so sorry for what I did."

Jade poured the salt onto the man's legs and he screamed and trembled as if fifty-thousand volts of electricity were flowing into him. The bed rocked and swayed, creaked and moaned. His head whipped back and forth. The vomit on his belly was tossed about, decorating the rest of the bed and floor and walls. Jade and the others kept back until the man settled down.

"Oh, I almost forgot one of my favorite parts of the movie," Jade said. She picked up the electric knife, went over to the dead woman and cut off her face. She made sure to peel it off carefully, not wanting to rip the eye holes.

Happy with her work, she came to a passed out Bud and stuck the wet skin mask to Bud's face. "I think I finally have a true indication of how Leatherface feels. Beautiful."

"Nice touch, babe," Daemon said.

"Thanks."

Bud was woken when Jade yanked out Bud's big-toe's nail. Then over the next couple of hours, the torture continued. Bud went in and out of consciousness, and seemingly in and out of reality. He'd clearly lost his mind when Jade crushed his left testicle with a pair of pliers, doing the same to the right one shortly after. The finale was when she sliced his flaccid penis in half and nailed each piece to his inner thigh. He'd shit the bed and puked a few more times by then, Jade disregarding the matter on her hands and shirt. She was having too much fun to let anything stop her.

"I think he's dead," Daemon said, feeling for a pulse.

"Good, I'm tired," Bobby said. "Sun's coming up. Can we go now?"

"All right," Jade said. "But before we leave I just wanted to thank you both for allowing me to do this, and have all the damn fun."

"I had some fun too," Bobby said. "Those two kills weren't too bad, despite someone's interfering . . ."

"He hurt you, babe," Daemon said. "And no one hurts you. You deserved this."

"Aww, babe, that means so much. It's one of the nicest things you've ever said to me." She came over to Daemon and open-mouth kissed him, making sure not to touch him with any other part of her.

"Okay, before you two screw in this filth, you guys need to clean yourselves up and we need to leave," Bobby said, heading to the door.

Bobby searched the premises for flammable liquids while Jade washed off in the shower. Her soiled clothes were piled on Bud's stomach. Gasoline from the gas can in the garage was splashed around the bedroom and living room before the bedroom was set ablaze. On the way out, the gas stove was turned on without flame, letting the gas fill the house. When they reached the Camry a few minutes later, the explosion rocked the airwaves.

Daemon and the others hopped into the car and drove away, taking an out of the way route to Bobby's. There was no real reason but to simply make it that much more difficult to put a trail from Bud's place to Bobby's.

"I can't wait to get home and—" Bobby began.

"Check it out, peeps," Jade said excitedly as she pointed ahead at the kid riding his bike alongside the road.

"No," Bobby said. "We're going straight home. No road kills until the troopers leave town."

"Dude, we have to," Daemon said, slowing the car. "There ain't no one around."

"We'll make it quick," Jade said.

"Too risky," Bobby said. "We haven't been listening to the scanner and the car isn't camouflaged."

"We'll be fine," Daemon said. "It's early. A quick lop off of the kid's head and we're done."

"Since I'm in the batter's seat and Bobby's outvoted ..." Jade reached into the back and laid her hand on the handle of the machete. Leaving it there, she looked up at Bobby. "What, you aren't going to stop me?"

"Like I could," he said.

Jade cackled, drew the machete to her, and faced forward.

The rider was wearing a white and blue bike helmet with a fin on top. Hanging off the rear bike rack was what looked like a long CB antenna.

"Looks like a real dorkmobile," Jade said. "Pull alongside the kid." Daemon sped up until Jade was even with the bicyclist. "Hey cutie," she said as she hung out the window.

Daemon kept pace with the boy.

"Hello," the boy said and kept pedaling.

"Are you a virgin?" Jade asked.

The kid moved a little ahead of the car. Daemon pressed the gas a tad more.

"You sure don't look like a virgin," Jade continued. "You're a sexy big boy, right?"

The kid ignored her, faced forward and pedaled.

"Want to see my tits?" Jade said and lifted her shirt and bra.

The kid didn't look.

"Must be a fag then," Jade said, pulled down her shirt, then grabbed the machete from the car and thrust it into the bike's front spokes. The machete clattered around for a second before catching when it came to the bike's fork. The front wheel ceased rotating. The back end lifted off the ground and then over the kid's head. He crashed headfirst to the asphalt, the bike tumbling ahead.

As the Camry passed the downed biker, Daemon hit the brakes and sent Jade into the door where the passenger side mirror was located.

"What the hell, babe?" Jade complained. "Learn to drive."

"Seriously?" Daemon said. "You were supposed to be quick."

"Kid pissed me off. Wouldn't even glance at my rack."

"Get back there and finish him," Bobby said. "He saw us."

Daemon put the car in reverse and when they reached where the kid had fallen, he was nowhere to be found.

"Fuck, he's gone," Bobby yelled.

Daemon pulled the Camry over and the trio got out.

"I told you guys this was a bad idea," Bobby said.

"Shut up," Jade said.

"He couldn't have gone far," Daemon said and opened the car's trunk. He handed Jade her crossbow, then picked up his machete. The .45 was tucked into his waistband at the back of his pants.

The sound of branches breaking emanated from the forest. All three killers glanced that way, then took off in that direction and disappeared into the woods.

Daemon and the others walked swiftly, eyes peeled. They ducked under branches and went around thick foliage until Jade spotted the kid. "There, little shit's yellow shirt sticks out like a dick on a chick."

Chasing after the boy, they reached a small clearing. Their prey was almost across it. Jade raised her weapon, aimed and fired, sending an arrow into the back of the kid's right shoulder. He cried out and went down.

They reached him in seconds as he crawled forward, his yellow shirt soaked with blood. Daemon stepped on his ankle, stopping him. Jade ripped out the arrow, a spray of crimson misting the air. The boy screamed.

"Shut up," Jade spat, then pointed at the arrow and said, "Hey, look at that."

Daemon saw the meat hanging off the tri-tipped arrowhead. "Damn, that had to hurt."

"C'mon, we ain't got all day," Bobby said.

Jade put her crossbow down and flipped the kid onto his back. His face was wet with tears. He blinked hard, then stared into her eyes before looking at Daemon and then Bobby. "You shouldn't have run, you little shit." Jade plunged the arrowhead into the boy's leg. He cried out again, and she slapped him. "Noisy little fuck."

Bobby kept looking back the way they had come. "We don't have time for this. The car is visible. The bike is there too."

"Okay, we do this one together," Daemon said. He stood next to the crying kid, raised his machete, smiled and then brought it down on the boy's neck, severing it completely.

"Asshole, you said we were doing this together," Bobby said.

"I lied," Daemon said, laughing.

"You didn't want to do this at all, so don't complain," Jade said.

"Whatever, we need to leave, and next time we kill, I'm getting first dibs," Bobby said, then stabbed the kid in the chest four times while grunting.

"Feel better?" Jade asked, taking back her arrow.

"Not at all, but at least I got to pretend. Now let's get back to the car and go home."

Chapter Twenty-Six

Amber awoke twenty minutes before her alarm went off and decided to get up so she could eat breakfast with her family instead of her usual routine of rushing out of the house.

"What cosmic event happened that we garnered the pleasure of your presence?" her mother asked when she entered the kitchen.

"Ha. Ha."

"Seriously, what brings you down here so early?"

"Can't I want to spend time with my family without a reason?"

"Of course you can, but you picked the wrong morning today."

"I see that," Amber said, looking at the empty set of chairs around the kitchen table.

"Dad had to leave early for a meeting," her mom said as she flipped over the omelet she was making. "And your brother took his bike out. Don't know when he'll be back. You know him and his experiments."

"What, so I got up early for nothing?"

Amber's mother looked over her shoulder at Amber. "Um, I'm here. You can still sit and eat with me."

"Wait, he took his bike out? As in out on the road?"

"Yes."

"Are you crazy? There are killers about."

"Oh, relax," her mother said, sliding the omelet onto a plate. "He'll be fine. It's early. The killings mostly happen later in the day and at night. I bet the killers are fast asleep at this hour."

Amber couldn't believe how flippant her mother was being. "People are being slaughtered. There's no rhyme or reason. And you're acting like it's no big deal. Sounds like you couldn't care less."

Her mother approached the table and placed a plate with an omelet, home fries, and sausage on it in front of Amber. "Don't be stupid. Of course I care. But I'm not going to let those scumbags frighten me to the point where my son can't go out and play. They're no different from terrorists. You can't be afraid. Can't alter your life. Screw them."

"This is different. This is a known threat, not the possibility of one. If you knew terrorists were at a specific airport with weapons, I sure bet you wouldn't go there or let a loved one go there until they were apprehended."

Her mom exhaled. "Amber, you're being too dramatic." The woman turned and went back to the stove.

Amber saw an inkling of doubt creep into her mother's mind. "No, I'm not being dramatic. You letting him go out at a time like this was bad parenting, but besides that, I can't believe he wasn't smart enough not to know not to go out." Amber felt herself growing angry, and not wanting to say something she regretted or hear The Voice, she shuffled egg into her mouth and chewed. Staying the course of not allowing herself to get angry and lose control was part of how she was healing herself and killing The Voice. She had an appointment next week with a therapist and wanted to be better so she would be that much farther along in her healing process.

Her mother didn't say anything else as she washed the frying pan. The woman was probably trying to compose herself, so she and Amber didn't get into a fight.

Amber went on eating her breakfast, downed the orange juice she'd poured for herself and got up from the table, putting her dish in the sink.

"You know, I just wanted to talk," her mother said. "You and me. It would have been nice."

"If you hadn't let him go out, then we could have, but I'm too pissed right now. Besides, I have to get going or I'll be late. I'll try to get up early tomorrow and we can try again. Hopefully, everyone will be here."

Amber grabbed her car keys and left.

A few hours later, she received a slightly frantic call from her mother telling her that Jason hadn't come home yet and wasn't answering his phone. She was getting worried. She also yelled at Amber for putting horrible thoughts in her head. "You've got me willy-nilly," she said.

Amber's heart raced and felt as if it had lodged in her throat. What if something had happened to Jason? No, she couldn't think like that. The kid was just out and doing his thing.

"Amber?"

"Yeah, I'm here."

"Did you hear what I said?"

She didn't know what to say. Part of her wanted to act nonchalant and tell her not to worry. Make the woman eat her own words. Another part of her wanted to berate her mom and tell her that's what you get for letting him out. Instead, she reeled herself in and said, "I'm sure he's fine." The words felt hollow. If she couldn't believe them herself, how could she expect her mother to believe them? Her gut churned. She was worried, wanted to run out of work and go look for him. Shit, that's what she should've done in the first place. Left this morning and went to find him, pick him up and bring him home.

"It's not like him not to answer his phone when I call," her mother said. "He always picks up."

"He'll show up soon. Maybe he lost his phone, or the battery went dead."

Or maybe he's the one who went dead.

"Shut up," she said.

"What?" her mother asked.

"Not you, mom. Look, I'm sure he's okay. He's just lost in one of his experiments—like you said."

"He said he'd be back in two hours or so. You know how precise he likes to be."

He's DEAD. DEAD. DEAD. And you know it.

Amber had slipped up when she told The Voice to shut up. She wasn't doing that again, wasn't going to acknowledge it. But it was getting difficult to control her anger. "You said he'd be fine, so deal with it." She hung up, unable to deal with it herself. Despite the din of the packed dining room, she heard nothing now. Slipping her phone back into her pocket, she realized she had no feeling in her limbs. In her body. Her mind went blank, all thought erased. For a moment, she wondered if she was dying. She didn't care one way or another.

Some amount of time passed. It couldn't have been more than a few seconds, but she wasn't sure. Finally, the jumble of noise from the multiple mouths talking entered her ears. Sensation came back into her body and her mind's gears began working again. Besides feeling frightened for her brother, she felt bad for how she treated her mom.

Bitch deserved it.

Amber shook her head. The only solution to her current problems was to focus on work. Block all else out. She took ten deep breaths, felt a little lightheaded, and then returned to work.

Her mother called back an hour later, but she didn't answer. Then the calls came in every twenty minutes. Amber refused to pick up. The constant calls made concentrating on her job and blocking out terrible thoughts difficult. Every time she felt herself breaking down and panic coming on, she made sure to talk to the customers or staff. A couple of times, people asked her if something was wrong. She'd simply force a smile and say no. She had to keep telling herself her brother was fine too, and that this would be a great lesson for her mother. The woman would think twice before letting Jason out again, at least until the killers were caught.

By the time her shift was nearing its end, her phone rang. It was her father. The man hardly called her. A tightness fell across her throat. She didn't want to pick up, but did, doing so quickly.

"Dad, what's up?" she asked, trembling inside.

"You need to come home, Amber," he said. His voice sounded grave.

Time seemed to freeze again. There was no more doubt that something was wrong. In fact, something terrible had happened. It didn't take a genius to figure out what it most likely was.

She left immediately, without punching out or telling anyone. She allowed for little thought and was instead on some kind of autopilot. The Voice was loose, saying awful things as she drove. She couldn't ignore it, but kept her thoughts to herself. At least she hoped they were to herself. For all she knew, The Voice knew all.

When she arrived home, she saw a police car parked in her driveway.

CHAPTER TWENTY-SEVEN

JASON WAS DEAD. HE had become another notch on the belts of the killers. His body had been found shortly after 4 p.m.

With Amber refusing to answer her phone, her mother had called the police. Normally, there would have to have been a twenty-four-hour period for Jason to be missing before the police would act, but taking into account what was happening around town, as well as Amber's mom being friends with the chief, they put a trace on his phone, locating it in the small clearing where he lay beheaded.

The Voice had been relentless up until the funeral. For some reason it had been quiet that day. Amber still felt its presence, but it remained quiet. It was giving her one day of peace to mourn. It wasn't enough. Not by a long shot.

The day after the funeral, The Voice was relentless again.

You must find the fuckers who slaughtered Jason and put them down. Kill them like they killed so many others. Whatever it takes. Get on a bike and act as bait. Buy a gun and shoot them all dead if you can't torture them. Cut off their heads and stuff their genitals in them. Stick those stuffed heads on poles at the edges of town, letting all killers know that this town is protected.

Amber listened to The Voice, if for anything, so she wouldn't go crazy with angst. She was given the week off from work. Working would have been good to occupy her mind, but with The Voice so present and uncontrollable, she couldn't take the chance.

Everything she ate came back up. Sleep was impossible. Jason plagued her nightmares. He was angry, blaming her for not finding him before the killers had. He was irate that Amber had not yet killed their mother, for it was ultimately the woman's fault he was dead. If she'd done her job as a parent, he'd be alive.

As soon as Amber woke from such nightmares, The Voice was there to add to the heartache and terror.

Day after day, she felt like a useless piece of garbage. There was nothing she could do to find the killers. The Voice claimed it could, that it would certainly find them. But that was bullshit, just an excuse to give in to it. How easy that would be to do. If she gave in, she might never return.

No one had entered Jason's room since the police left the house except for when Amber's mom had to get clothes for the wake and funeral. Everyone had been surprised there would be a viewing considering the brutal way Jason was killed, but the funeral parlor made it appear as if Jason had never been decapitated.

Amber needed to enter the room. Needed to be as close to her brother as was possible. He was gone, but being surrounded by his things would be something. A something that was better than nothing.

After gathering up the courage, she went into his room and closed the door behind her. There, she cried and cried and cried as she hugged his clothes and went through his things. Seeing his broken drone made her angry, made her wish she'd hurt those bullying kids.

The rage didn't last.

Jason's smell was everywhere, and she loved it. She wanted it in her clothes and to never fade. If only she could hear his voice. That would make her feel better. There had to be a recording of it somewhere. Maybe even videos. She thought for a moment and remembered there was a video on her phone. It was in her room. She didn't want to leave yet. Once she left, she wasn't sure she could come back. Not for a while. As much as she loved being in his room, the pain she would feel when she left would destroy her for a time. Her eyes settled on his laptop. Maybe there was a video there.

Sitting at his desk, she lifted the computer's lid and pressed the power button. The device came to life, the SSD drive making the boot time seconds. As she studied his desktop screen, a video file downloaded. It must have been something Jason had sent to his laptop from another device, but having not turned on the machine, it never had the chance to download.

She'd completed one of his last actions, something he'd wanted to see but would never get the chance to.

A chill ran through her.

She needed to know what it was. Something funny, important or a video of one of his experiments. That would be wonderful because she wanted to see and hear him again, if only for a few moments.

She found the download folder, clicked it open, and then clicked on the video file.

The screen came to life. The image was of Jason's face. He was talking to the camera on his helmet. She turned up the volume and heard him say how he was going to record his morning bike ride, and when he played it back, he was going to see what he missed when reviewing the video. Some kind of observation experiment.

The camera view changed to one of the road. Then he started moving. He looked at his feet, his hands, the trees alongside the road, the sky and straight ahead, repeating this motion every so often. He stopped the bike at one point and focused the camera on a dead and rotting raccoon. The animal corpse was on its back, half its bones showing on one side. Where there was fur, it rippled. *Maggots*, Amber thought, and shivered.

The same maggots now blooming inside Jason, hungering for his flesh. They'll eat him down to the bones, you know?

She ignored The Voice, and after thirty seconds of camera time, Jason continued on. The video was monotonous. Boring even. Jason wasn't speaking, and she was only rewarded with occasional views of his hands and feet. But she continued to watch, hoping for another glimpse of his face and voice. Then, at the thirty-two-minute mark, a vehicle pulled alongside him. A young woman with purple hair was hanging out the window and speaking to him. Amber immediately recognized her as Jade Rawlings. She had been two grades ahead of Amber in high school and a real loser. A wild girl who was in detention as much as she was in class. A girl who was constantly getting into fistfights with students on a regular basis, and then there were the times she wasn't seen because she had been suspended, which was often. Looking beyond Jade, Amber saw the driver, Daemon Winters. The two had been going out in high school and she wasn't surprised to see that they were still together. The pair of low lives were made for each other.

As the scene progressed, Amber's skin prickled. Her insides felt as if they were shrinking. Something wasn't right. Her brain connected what she was watching to the killings around town, and then to Jason's death.

A lightning strike of unease shot through her. It couldn't be true. Jade and Daemon were bad kids, but killers?

Jason was now looking straight ahead, and she was happy he wasn't giving them the satisfaction. But a few seconds later, the scene went haywire as if the camera had gone tumbling away.

Not the camera, stupid. Jason.

Amber was sitting forward, fingers gripping the arms of the chair like an eagle gripping its fresh catch. Tears streaked her face, and she tasted blood, her teeth having broken flesh. She watched as her brother's view focused on the car, then moved into the woods. He was running and crying. Though she knew it was pointless, she rooted for him to get away.

He went down, crying out in obvious pain.

Voices of his attackers filled her ears.

Then she saw them. Three people surrounded Jason—Jade, Daemon and Bobby Lancaster. The three rotten amigos. No, they were way more than that. They were evil. Local evil who had never bothered her but had caused plenty of havoc for others.

She watched Jade stab her brother as tears streaked her face.

Then Daemon raised a machete and—

She turned away, unable to watch. But it didn't matter. Her mind produced the images.

Her stomach churned.

They cut off his little, bitty head.

Amber couldn't stop herself and hurled her stream of vomit just making it into the wastebasket under the desk. Sitting up, she clicked off the video and screamed for as long and as loud as possible, hurting her own ears. She screamed until her throat bled, the taste of copper rich on her palate.

The room tilted as she stood. The air was too thin. Amber couldn't breathe. She needed out of the room, took a step forward and tripped over a pair of shoes. She landed hard, stayed there and cried until there were no more tears.

A loud silence like she'd never experienced surrounded her.

You know what you have to do.

Amber did and pushed herself up. A mirror attached to the wall on her right displayed her twin. Her eyes were cracked with red, face shiny with tears. Disgusted by her weakness, she wiped them away.

Unable to stare at herself anymore, she looked at the laptop. She could hand the device over to the police and let the justice system have its way with them. They would surely be arrested. Taken off the street and locked away forever.

You sure about that? That video doesn't actually show them kill him. Maybe they'll say they only scared him by swinging the machete close to his face. A good, expensive lawyer will get them so they only have to serve a few years, or at worst, get them off entirely. Bobby is wealthy. His parents would never allow him to go away for the rest of his life. They would be out before you know it. Time flies when you're having fun. They'll be able to ruin more people's lives because once a psycho killer, always a psycho killer. You need to do to them what you couldn't do to Rex.

"You're right," she said. "But I'm not a killer. I couldn't, possibly .. . I wouldn't ......"

Enough with this bullshit. You are a pussy. You've proved that. That's why I'm here. I can do what needs to be done. Let me be your sword, your vengeance. Those animals must pay. The justice system is broken, and at best a gamble. You can't allow the cops to be involved. Only you can end them. End all the suffering they will surely bring. Stand up for the victims, for Jason, for yourself.

The Voice was correct. She had done nothing about Rex. Let him run her out of town. Left him to rape other women. She couldn't allow more rotten apples to go on doing evil things.

"Okay," she said, knowing it was time to let The Voice in.

Chapter Twenty-eight

MUCH OF AMBER WAS gone. She'd given in to The Voice, the part of herself that frightened her, but at the same time would allow her to do what needed to be done. She liked to think of it as her warrior self, but The Voice was more than that. It was malicious, a killer. It reveled in what it wanted to do to others. Killing wasn't going to be enough. It wanted those who wronged her to suffer. There was something in the prolonged pain of her enemies that brought a great sense of justice and satisfaction. It wasn't the norm. Wasn't what she had been taught or what most of society believed on the surface. But deep down, all humans were capable of evil. But what she was going to do wasn't pure evil, was it? There were not going to be random acts of violence. The Voice promised focus and meaning.

After the deeds were done, she could only hope to return to some kind of normalcy. Return to a semblance of who she had been.

Killing isn't wrong when it's for a good reason, The Voice had told her. *If someone was coming at you with a knife and planned on killing you, would you curl up and die? No, you'd pull out your gun, if you had one, and blast the fucker, killing them to protect yourself. By killing those who hurt others, you are taking preventative steps in ensuring less pain and heartache.*

It was right after that when Amber gave in completely and changed, her mind becoming darker and her view of the world cynical. Gone was the sunshine and thoughts of a bright future, replaced by the need for immediate action and death.

If she had to face the truth, she knew she was not coming back, regardless of her previous positive thinking. And if that was the case, she'd be okay with it. Just like she had to be okay with how Jason was never coming back.

The first thing Amber did was gather a cache of weapons, buying a 12-gauge shotgun and sawing off the stock and cutting down the barrel, making it a much more concealable weapon. She also purchased a ski mask, hunting knife, and a smaller boot-knife she could strap to her ankle. Acquiring a stun gun proved more difficult than the other tools. She had to drive to Pennsylvania where she bought one.

She returned to work a week after Jason's funeral, wanting to keep up as normal an Amber appearance as possible. It was difficult to act like her old self with The Voice demanding she act against all who abused her in any way, from the customer who called her honey to the woman who left her a fifty-cent tip, to the teenagers who made lewd comments under their breath. But with her cunning, she convinced The Voice to focus only on Jade, Daemon and Bobby.

Amber felt cold inside, as if she were the embodiment of a living meat-cooler—even in the hot summer sun. She was never happy or sad. Her demeanor was even-keeled or angry, the anger always present to some degree and in never-ending supply. The raw emotion was fuel for The Voice and Amber made sure to keep the pump flowing.

There were times when she had to remove herself from a situation. If a customer was rude, she'd go out back and swear like a whore at a truck stop. When she was in her car and was cut off, or she got caught behind someone moving too slowly, she'd holler and swear while punching the seat next to her. If she was home alone, she'd kick and punch her bed, pillows and anything else in her path.

Keeping her emotions bottled up was impossible. Release was necessary.

At night when she was lying in bed, her parents at home, she would scream into her pillow if needed. Or tense up all her muscles and hold her breath until she thought she would pass out, and then breathe again.

In between gathering her weapons, she also found out where each of her brother's killers lived. She visited each address, taking pictures and studying the layout as well as any routines. They were together most of the time and hung out at Bobby's house. She'd seen no sign of his parents and guessed they were either dead or on vacation. Other times, Daemon and Jade would leave to spend the night at Daemon's, and since she'd been watching, Jade had yet to go home.

It came down to her parking a mile from Bobby's house, creeping up to the tree line that ran along the backyard by the pool, and listening. There, the killers got high night after night and talked; the scum rehashing with glee about their kills, including Jason's—and each time his name was mentioned, it took everything she had not to charge the group blasting away.

But that wasn't part of the plan.

For the fifth night in a row, the trio was hanging out by the pool around the fire pit, getting high and bullshitting. Amber was growing tired of waiting, her patience thin like a sheet of paper. She figured Daemon and Jade would eventually leave to sleep in their own beds.

Why would they want that when they have a mansion to fuck in?

Amber agreed.

It really was starting to look like the murderous couple would never leave. She couldn't wait forever. Attacking all three was too risky. They all needed to die, and die knowing why they were targets. Attacking recklessly would most likely lead to one or two of them surviving and her being put in the ground.

Growing increasingly agitated, biting her nails down to flesh, she watched as Daemon and Jade rose from their chairs, told Bobby they'd see him tomorrow, then head to Daemon's car and leave.

The long-haired killer remained in his chair by the pool, his back to her.

Amber salivated with the kill opportunity and crept from the foliage and across the lawn with the stun gun in hand. There was no way she could climb over the fence that surrounded the pool without being heard, and no way could she enter from the gate without him seeing her.

Standing at the fence directly behind Bobby, she tucked the stun gun into her pants at the small of her back and said, "Hello."

Bobby jumped out of his chair and spun toward her. "What the hell, girl . . ." He was breathing hard. "You scared the shit out of me."

"Sorry about that," Amber said, her insides brimming with joy.

"Where'd you come from?"

"I was out walking, saw your fire, and figured I'd see who was hanging out so late."

"You live around here?"

"No, I'm visiting my aunt. Got bored."

"You always bring a backpack with you on your walks?"

"No, but my little cousin is a snoop and a thief. Can't leave my private things around or they might go missing."

Bobby's eyes kept darting into the darkness behind her.

He's looking to see if you're alone.

"Are you by yourself?" Bobby asked, focusing on her.

"Yeah, why?" The guy was nervous. Being cautious. It was understandable.

"Just checking. Can't be too careful these days." His shoulders fell a little. He seemed to relax. "My friends already left, but I've got beer and weed."

"A beer sounds good," she said, hoping to sound sexy.

"Come around through the gate," Bobby said, motioning with his arm.

Amber swallowed and felt the lump in her throat. She was nervous, but at the same time, her pulse was quick, and she was excited. Excited to tie this little piggy up and make him squeal. Slow and steady. She couldn't screw this up.

She entered the pool area and walked over to where Bobby was sitting. She reached back and touched the stun gun, not pulling it out. Bobby reached into the cooler and withdrew a beer, the icy water cascading off the can like sweat from a marathon runner. She feigned taking the beverage while pulling the stun gun free with her other hand, when he lunged out of his chair and punched her in the face.

White lightning flashed across her vision as her head jerked sideways. The rest of her body followed,, and she stumbled over the lawn chair behind her. She twisted mid-fall, trying to right herself, and put out her arms to brace for impact. Instinct took over right before she hit the cement. Her fingers opened, palms ready to take the brunt of the impact, but in doing so, lost the stun gun. The device tumbled a few feet away.

"Stupid bitch," Bobby said.

She fast-crawled forward and reached out for the stun gun when she was grabbed by her backpack from behind. Unable to move forward, she kicked back like a frightened horse and connected with something solid. Her attacker swore, but held onto her. Pulling the backpack straps off her shoulders, she slid her arms free. Momentum carried her forward, inches from the stun gun. Reaching for the weapon, she saw Bobby's boot land on her hand and pin it in place. The pressure increased, the killer grinding her fingers against the hard surface. Fire-like angst enveloped her hand and shot up her arm.

"Should have brought a real gun, sweetheart," Bobby said. "You wouldn't have had to get so close."

She batted at his leg with her fist, her mind in a frenzy.

Get your knife, stupid, and sink it into his fucking flesh.

Before she could reach down to her ankle, Bobby removed his foot, grabbed her by her shoulders, and flipped her onto her back. A second later, he was sitting on her, pinning her arms to the ground with his.

"Did you think I wouldn't recognize you?" he said. "I research everyone we kill, for instances just like this. Should someone come a-knocking, I'll be prepared. You're that little twat's sister, Amber Marshall."

He released her right wrist, only to punch her in her gut. The wind was knocked out of her and she struggled to draw breath.

"What was your plan?" He backhanded her, and she tasted blood. "Were you going to hurt me? Fuck me up a little before you called the cops?" He shook his head. "No, I don't think so. You weren't planning on cops, were you? If that was the case, you could've just told them about us. Somehow you found out about us and wanted to gather intel. Evidence. You got a recorder on you?"

He began feeling her up, asking her where she hid the wire. She struck out with her right hand and clawed his face. "Cunt," he said and backhanded her so hard she blacked out.

She came to with him rifling through her backpack. She was sitting up, slumped over. "I know you got something in here . . . What the hell?"

He'd discovered her items.

"Crazy bitch was planning on torturing me? Damn."

She remained still. Needed to fool him.

"Bah, no recording device," he said, then pulled the backpack off her and laid her on her side. Eyes closed, she felt his hand slide down her shirt. His touch was serpent-like, bringing a frigid chill to her bones.

Time to party.

Opening her eyes, she bolted upright, grabbed his head, and clamped her teeth down onto his cheek. Like a starved lion, she shook her head to free the meat. Bobby screamed. His sour blood filled her mouth. He tried pushing her away, but her jaw was locked on the flesh like a Pit Bull's. Her teeth severed more flesh.

It will be yours soon.

"Fucking cunt," Bobby yelled as he tried batting her away.

As she continued to gnaw, she reached down, pulled up her pant leg, and grabbed the handle of the boot-knife she kept latched to her ankle. Sliding the weapon free, she brought it up and jabbed it into Bobby's side. She felt him weaken immediately, his blows becoming soft like a de-clawed cat's. With a grunt of triumph, she shoved him away, keeping a chunk of cheek-meat with her. He fell back and to the ground, a pulpy, bleeding hole in his face.

Amber spit out the meat and turned toward the stun gun. Snatching it up, she went to stand and was wrapped up in a bear hug. Bobby lifted her off the ground, turned her sideways, and then threw her down. Putting out her arms, she had to let go of the weapons she held, the stun gun and knife no longer under her control. The impact was jolting. Her knees smashed against unyielding concrete, and she cried out.

"You're fucking dead," Bobby growled and stomped her back, then kicked her in her side. Having no time to regain her senses, she was flipped onto her back. Bobby climbed onto her; the right side of his shirt bloodied. He used his legs to spread hers while he held her wrists down. "But first I'm going to fuck you up so badly you'll beg me to kill you." He released his grip on her arms, sat up and punched her across the face before backhanding her head the other way. Stars exploded across her vision as pain weaved its way deep into her head.

Fighting through the attack, she said, "Fuck you" but a moment later, could no longer breathe. Bobby's hands were clutching her throat, squeezing it closed. Her head was lifted a few inches off the ground and then slammed back down. Bobby continued to strangle her, the pain from her head being bashed a far second on her list of things to be concerned about.

She was going to die.

No, you aren't.

Amber pounded at her attacker's arms, but it was like hitting steel. Her vision was fading. Her body needed oxygen. All she'd planned and gone through, and she was going to be done in by one of her brother's killers.

Like a supernatural force, anger overpowered her fear in seconds. She dug her nails into Bobby's forearms and let loose a silent scream of fury. He swore, released his hold on her and grabbed her by her hair. Lifting her head off the ground, he then slammed his fist squarely into her nose. Her head shot back and hit the cement with a brain-rattling thud. She heard him clear his throat and spit before feeling his warm phlegm. "You ruined my face."

His hands were around her throat again, choking her. He slammed her head again. If she didn't do something soon, she was going to die.

DO SOMETHING!

Bobby released his hold again, and she sucked in a breath. "Don't worry, cunt, I ain't going to kill you so quickly. First, I'm going to have some fun with you. Fuck you silly. Fill your ass with my dick and make you cry like the cunt you are." His hands went to her chest, and he pinched her nipples. The pain was electric, but it helped focus her hate and power. She wouldn't react again. Wouldn't give the sick motherfucker the satisfaction.

"Guess you like that," he said, and let go of her nipples. "Going to have a lot of fun with you, it seems." He smacked her head right, then to the left, and then she saw the stun gun. It lay an arm's length away. She needed to distract him and get to it.

"Word is you have a small dick," she said, laughing.

Bobby smiled. "Oh, yeah? I'll show you how small my dick is, but first," using his right hand, he punched her in her stomach, then launched a follow up left to her jaw. Her head swirled, and she felt blackness coming on. Another blow and she would surely wake up to the pig raping her.

That couldn't happen.

Forget the stun gun. You are an animal.

She lay there, pretending to be unconscious. Eyes closed, she hoped another blow wasn't coming. Instead, she received a gentle slap. "C'mon. Wakey, wakey." He slapped her harder. "Hey, cunt. Wake up."

She mumbled, making sure it was nothing coherent.

"What was that?"

She mumbled again; her face throbbing and achy.

He leaned closer and cocked his ears forward with his hands. "What was that, cunt? Going to have to speak up."

NOW!

Amber reached up, grabbed onto his head, and sunk her thumbs into his eye sockets. The orbs burst as her fingernails punctured the gelatinous, fluid-filled spheres. Bobby screamed. Warm goo covered her digits. Amber withdrew her flesh-daggers and pushed Bobby off her. Reaching over, she snatched up the stun gun, jumped onto a wailing, eyeless Bobby and zapped him into unconsciousness.

Chest heaving, face bruised, and bloody fingers caked in gore, she opened her backpack, got out the handcuffs and secured Bobby's hands behind his back. She then taped his ankles together using her duct tape. Though he was blinded, she wasn't taking any more chances.

Wake and drown him.

"Not yet," she said, then donned her black ski mask, making sure to tuck in her long blonde hair. After duct-taping his mouth closed, she searched Bobby's pockets and found his phone. Setting it to camera mode, she then positioned it on a chair facing Bobby. The fire pit's flames cast the man in a perfect light.

After hitting record, she got the ball-peen hammer from her backpack and returned to Bobby's side. Looking into the camera, she smiled, then brought the nail-pounding tool down on Bobby's right knee.

CRACK!

Amber felt the spherical bone shatter, the sound popping. Bobby screamed and writhed; his cries muffled by the gag. "Shush. It'll be all right. Don't you worry none." She raised the hammer and bashed his other kneecap.

CRACK!

Bobby screamed again and sat up, snot leaking from his nostrils and spittle drooling from the gag. Tears mixed with blood from his eyeless sockets streaked his face, the liquid glistening in the fire's light. Amber wanted to hit him in the face, but instead shoved him down and went back to work, smashing his right shin.

Grinding her teeth, the giddiness she'd been feeling left, replaced by rage. Up and down the hammer went, the blows as hard as she could make them. Bone broke and splintered, Bobby's pant legs shredded and bloody. When she reached his ankles, she pulverized the bony knobs on each one.

Bobby had thrown up, the upchuck spurting from his gag, the rest she guessed he was able to swallow back down. She hadn't thought of the possibility he would puke and hoped he wouldn't suffocate, but she wasn't about to let him soil her. Get his blood on her—sure, but not his bile.

Finished with his lower body, she cracked his elbows, turning the pointy protrusions into rubble and bleeding skin. Bobby begged for his life, tossed his head back and forth to the point where she thought he'd snap his own neck, and wondered if he was trying to do just that.

Vomit continued to spew, the gag soaked and wet and thinner.

Good, we don't want him dying on us yet, do we?

"No, we don't."

After shattering his arms, she broke each of his fingers by bending and twisting them in ways they weren't meant to be. When she was finished, his hands resembled the bristles of a worn-out grill brush, the metal strands curved and no longer uniform.

Satisfied with her work, she got up, went over to the cell phone and clicked off the camera, then sent the video to Daemon's phone.

Chapter Twenty-nine

After intense buckets of-sweat-inducing sex that ended with Daemon shooting his load onto Jade's tits before she licked them clean, the couple lay back on the bed and shared a cigarette. They made small talk and before long were getting ready to fuck again when Daemon's phone chimed, indicating he had a message from Bobby.

Since they had begun their killing spree, the group always made sure they were able to reach each other, and never left a phone call or message unchecked for long.

Reaching out to the nightstand, he unplugged his cell phone from the charger and looked at the screen. "Well, check this out. Bobby sent me a video."

"Awww, the bag of bones misses us already," Jade said, expelling smoke from her lungs.

"Probably got so drunk, he ass-videoed," Daemon said, laughing. He clicked on the file and the video played. His flesh went cold at seeing Bobby tied up and a masked figure next to him. He hoped it was a joke, but quickly saw it was not when Bobby screamed.

Jade sat up, her nipples like rods of steel. "What are you watch—" Jade sucked in a breath. "Is that Bobby?"

Daemon nodded, unable to speak.

"Holy shit. Is this a joke?" Jade asked.

Daemon didn't answer her, watching the video intensely. The scene unfolding before him was brutal, and the last thing he'd ever expected. His stomach churned, half with hate, half with shock. His best friend was slowly being tortured to death. Even if Bobby managed to make it out of his situation, he'd never see, walk or use his hands the same again.

Daemon's stomach was in his groin. A heavy weight had fallen on top of him, and for the first time in numerous years, he felt sad. The emotion didn't remain long because his anger flared up. He was pissed that someone was hurting his friend, but even more pissed that he was vulnerable to such pain. He was soft. A pussy. It was bullshit. He was a hard-nosed killer.

Never having thought about losing his friend, he was hit with a wave of emotions he'd thought were long dead. What about Jade? He fucking loved her more than anything. They were soulmates destined to rule a small part of hell together. He'd do anything for her. That was also weakness. But it was one he'd have to be okay with because he knew she felt the same way. All others were worth less than the shit on the bottom of his boot. He thought no more about killing a person than an ant. Squash them both and move on, although killing a human brought a sense of satisfaction unfelt by anything else. And he got to share that with his soulmate.

"Babe, what are we going to do?" Jade asked, hugging him from behind. "This shit ain't right. We're the hunters, not whoever is in that video."

"I know."

"We need to find them and kill them. Like tonight."

"I know."

"So . . ."

"I don't know what to do." He was indecisive. Stalling and afraid. Someone knew about them and was intent on making them pay. It was the only explanation. He couldn't show fear, though, especially not to Jade. "But we're going to find the prick and make what he did to Bobby look like child's play."

Daemon and Jade got dressed. They took their handguns, but also loaded the crossbow, machete, and a few knives into the Camry's trunk. If they had the chance, they would prolong their enemy's suffering for as long as possible, but they were going in with the intent to kill first and foremost. If someone knew who they really were, it was best to end them quickly. The video was a message. It stated that the person had no intention of going to the cops. The gauntlet had been thrown down. This was going to be between himself, Jade and Bobby's torturer.

They drove to Bobby's house.

Daemon stopped the car halfway down the driveway, staying within the wooded section of the property so as not to alert Bobby's attacker if the guy was still present.

They exited the car, taking only their guns with them. When they reached the lawn, they went right and skirted along the tree line, avoiding the motion-sensing flood lights located on the front of the house. They then made their way to the backyard, surveyed the pool area, and waited just inside the tree line.

The fire still blazed in the fire pit. The pool lights were on, the bluish water sparkling. Various lights were on inside the house, too, casting more illumination into the backyard.

"No one here," Jade said.

"Asshole's probably hiding. Waiting."

"You think there's more than one person?"

Daemon shrugged. "No way to tell. Video showed one, but let's assume there are more."

"What about Bobby?"

"He's . . ." Daemon couldn't say it. "We'll help him when we find him."

"Do you think they know we're here?"

"Nah. We parked far enough away. No way anyone saw us sneaking back here."

"I hate to break it to you, babe, but there ain't no rush. Bobby's most likely already dead."

He turned on her. "Don't you think I know that? And if he isn't yet, he will be. You saw what that fucker did to him. They had no intention of him surviving."

"So why didn't they just kill him?"

"Cuz they want us to suffer. Must be related to someone we offed."

"We're going to really, really hurt whoever it is. They have no idea who they fucked with."

"No, they don't."

Forty-five minutes after arriving at the backyard, Daemon and Jade took turns smoking cigarettes to help pass the time, the smoker going a few feet deeper into the forest so as not to alert anyone to the glowing orange embers.

As more time passed—an hour, then two—Daemon was ready to explode. Jade paced and smoked twice as many cigarettes as him. He was no less angry, but was surprised at how patient he was able to be. But he was at his wit's end and decided to check out the house, figuring Bobby's torturer had left. Maybe even taken Bobby with him. The video message was just that, a message that they were going to have to watch their backs, and they were now the hunted.

"All right," he said, standing. "Enough of this shit. Let's go see what's what." He stepped out of the tree line, gun in hand. Jade was right behind him. He told her to go to the house and meet by the back porch. "Keep an eye out and cover me."

Daemon walked on, his head on a swivel as Jade headed off. When he reached the fence, he climbed over it in two movements, landing like a practiced thief. As he approached the table and chairs where the video had been shot, he saw a large bloody area by the side of the pool, the crimson streaking down the side and turning the water cherry red. It spread out into a pink-tinted cloud. Below it was a headless body resting on the bottom of the pool. It was Bobby. The fucker had cut off his head. Whoever they had pissed off was like them—willing to go to extremes.

A chill swept over him as he realized how vulnerable he was in the open area, lit up like a prison yard during an escape. He looked to his left and saw Jade standing by the sliding glass door that led into the house.

"Well?" she said.

"Stay there, I'm coming to you." He glanced around, looked at his headless dead friend. He was afraid. Didn't like being toyed with. His ears waited to hear a gunshot, some sniper having him in his sights. He'd feel the bullet hit him fractions of a second later. If it was a head shot, he would feel nothing—just be blinked out of existence.

Swallowing hard, he headed to where Jade was waiting.

"Bobby's dead."

Jade looked at him. "How do you—"

"His headless body's in the pool."

"Fuck. They took his head?"

"Yeah."

"I'm so sorry, babe. I know he was like a brother to you." She rubbed his arm. "We'll avenge him, for sure. Don't you worry."

"Damn right we will. "Let's check the house."

They headed inside and quickly went room to room. Nothing was out of order or messed up. It appeared that Bobby's killer had not gone into the house and had left the property. Maybe he was watching them. Waiting to strike.

"This sucks," Jade said after guzzling a beer from the fridge. "Motherfucker's playing games with us."

"Exactly. He wants us to fear him. Turn our own game on us. But screw that. We are fear."

"I think we should leave. Maybe the cops are on their way. First, we got to wipe our prints from this place."

"We're friends and have been in this house more than our own over the last month. Our prints and DNA are everywhere. It would be odd if our shit wasn't here. Hell, I blew my load on his mom's pillow last week, remember?"

"Hell yeah, I remember. Half went on my face. You usually never miss my mouth by that much."

"I was wasted."

Daemon would normally have taken her at that moment, but he wasn't right. The whole situation they were in had screwed him up. The tables had turned, and he didn't like it at all.

"We should leave anyway," Jade said. "No reason to be here. If the cops show, what, you want to chat with them?"

"I don't know what to do. I can't think straight. So fucking pissed. But there's no doubt the cops will come looking for us. We'll say we were here but left him alone. It's the truth, anyway."

"Right. Now let's go home. We know someone's after us, so we'll be ready. They really fucked up by letting us know about them."

Daemon wasn't so sure. The killer wanted them off their game, their confidence destroyed. Jade was crazier. She might be fine. He was rattled.

No, fuck that. He wasn't going to let some hiding-in-the-shadows douche bag alter his being. "First thing we need is money. With Bobby gone, our cash cow is gone."

"You see," Jade said, throwing up her arms. "We never should've relied on him for money. We had plenty of chances to get our own."

"I don't want to hear it, Jade," Daemon shouted, then walked past her, into the hallway and up the stairs. Jade followed, swearing at him for cutting her off. He apologized, and then they searched the room for Bobby's go-bag, a backpack full of $100,000 dollars, finding it easily in the back of his walk-in closet. "Now we can go."

They left via the back door and hurried down the driveway to the car. Daemon opened the driver's side door and froze as his eyes settled on Bobby's severed head resting on his chair. "Fuck." He slammed his fist on the car's roof. He pulled out his .45.

"What?" Jade asked and peered through the passenger side window.

"Guy's been here all along."

Daemon lifted the head by its long, stringy hair and tossed it away.

Jade spun around and faced the wooded area, gun out. Daemon did the same on his side of the car and scanned the surrounding area, seeing only inky woods and driveway. Something in his mind told him to check the tires. He glimpsed the front one and swore. Looking at the back tire, he saw the same thing. "Fucker slashed the tires." He pounded the side of the car with his fist.

"Car will still drive, only slower," Jade said. Keeping her eyes on the woods, she reached back, opened the door and climbed in.

Daemon opened the trunk, grabbed an old rag he kept there and laid it on the seat to cover the blood. After sitting, he felt the cold crimson liquid soak into his jeans. Just wanting to leave, he ignored it and turned the key in the ignition, but to no avail. His foot pressed the gas pedal, and he tried again. Nothing. "Car's dead."

"We walk then," Jade said and was about to get out when Daemon grabbed her wrist.

"Wait here. I'm going to check the engine."

"Fuck that," she said, pulled away from him and opened her door.

Daemon let out a pent-up breath and was about to open his door when his mind flashed back to when he got the rag out of the trunk. Something had been different. Missing. Then it hit him—the crossbow was gone.

"Jade, get back in here now," he yelled.

She was standing and facing the car when her body jerked as if struck by something. A gasp escaped her lips, and she fell forward into the vehicle. An arrow was poking out of her lower back.

Daemon held her down with his free hand, extended his gun arm over her and fired into the woods. It was reactionary fire, but also cover fire. He emptied the magazine, let the gun fall to his lap, and helped pull Jade's legs into the car, then reached over and shut the door. Jade groaned with every movement she made.

He quickly loaded another magazine into his gun.

"Fuck, this hurts," Jade said, breathing shallowly. She couldn't sit properly due to the arrow and remained on her shins with her back to the passenger window.

"What do I do, pull it out?" Daemon asked.

"I don't know, but it kills."

"Fuck, fuck, fuck," Daemon screamed and punched the steering wheel. "I'm going to kill this motherfucker deader than dead."

Jade coughed and decorated the dashboard with blood. "That can't be good."

"We got to get you to a hospital, babe," Daemon said, his voice cracking. I've got to go outside and take care of this prick." He opened the door, and as he stepped out, was met with blinding pain.

CHAPTER THIRTY

Staying low like a lion ready to strike, Amber snuck up to the driver's side door and waited. As soon as Daemon stepped out, she pounced, pressing the stun gun to the back of his neck. He trembled as volts of electricity entered his body. The gun in his hand fell to the ground and his legs gave out. She held the weapon against him as he fell into the door, whacked his head, and then hit the driveway.

"Get away from him," Jade yelled.

Amber snatched up Daemon's gun as she heard the boom of a firearm, then felt the sting of a bullet as it grazed the back of her head. She pushed herself away as more gunshots sounded, the open door becoming riddled with holes. Glass shattered, and the shards rained down on an unconscious Daemon.

Got lucky there, toots. Got to be more careful.

Amber nodded her agreement with The Voice and crouched low near the rear tire as the gunfire ceased. She wanted to drag Daemon away and tie him up before he woke, but there was no way she was getting close enough without taking a bullet.

"Babe?" Jade yelled. "C'mon, you got to wake up."

Amber smiled, giddy inside to have brought worry and panic to such evil creatures. Let them experience what their victims and their victims' families had. Hearing the panic in Jade's voice was exactly what she and The Voice needed to hear. To her surprise, there was genuine concern for Daemon from Jade. Maybe even love. How people of such evil character could be capable of such a thing, she had no idea.

"Get up, babe," Jade continued.

"I've got a gun trained on your *babe*," Amber said, almost laughing. "Toss out your weapon or he dies."

"You're a fucking chick?" Jade said, laughing. "A chick did all this?" She kept laughing as if it was the funniest thing she'd heard in a long time. "Way to go. Girl Power all the way, dude."

Gunshots rang out, and the glass window above Amber exploded. Diamond-like fragments pelted her flesh, but no harm befell her.

Yay for safety glass.

Amber knew what she needed to do. Performing an about-face, she crouch-walked to the bumper, then to the other side of the vehicle, where she peered around the corner to the passenger side mirror. She hoped to get an image of Jade, but it was too dark. That was good. It meant she could most likely sneak up to the door unnoticed, especially if Jade was focused on Daemon and the other side of the car.

Keeping her left shoulder pressed against the car to stay as close to it as possible, she moved toward the passenger door. Jade was still pleading for Daemon to wake up.

Good, the bitch is distracted.

Hunkered next to the door, she grabbed the handle and paused.

What if it's locked?

"Then I'll shoot her through the glass and end her," Amber mumbled, wanting the woman alive so she could *deal* with her, but realizing the ultimate goal was to end them all and get out alive.

Taking a few quick breaths, she pulled on the handle and the door opened.

Jade's back was to her, the arrow still protruding from it. With the pronged tip, Amber knew short of going to a hospital there was no safe way to pull it out without causing more damage.

Jade tried to spin around and face her, but the arrow smacked against the seatback, preventing her from doing so. As the woman cried out, Amber grabbed the arrow and pressed the .45 she held to the back of Jade's head. "Move and I'll—"

Jade growled as she raised her gun arm up and over her shoulder. Amber's mouth fell open at the sheer lack of care for the woman's own safety. Almost caught off guard, having expected the woman to obey, she grabbed the arrow and jerked it around. The gun went off as Jade screamed. The bullet zipped by Amber's ear, missing it by millimeters.

Seeing Jade still holding onto the weapon, Amber yanked on the arrow and ripped it free. The gun went off again, sending a bullet into the roof of the vehicle as a stream of crimson spilled from the wound in Jade's back. The woman howled in obvious pain and dropped the gun. Amber then reached back and nailed Jade on the back of her neck as hard as she could with the butt of the .45. The woman went silent and slumped forward.

She stood there for a moment, catching her breath and thinking she had both killers ready to be hog-tied when she was grabbed by her hair and thrown backward. She hit the blacktop hard, her elbows and the back of her aching head taking the impact. Her vision went blurry as white-hot pain enveloped her skull. The gun was still in her grasp, but only for a moment when Daemon's boot connected with her hand. Amber's ring and pinky fingers snapped, and the gun went skidding away.

The sharp pain of her bones breaking was like a splash of cold water to her face, waking her from her dazed state. Eyesight clearing, she saw Daemon's boot coming toward her face, and then rolled to the side in time to avoid being stomped. Not taking a moment to think, she simply reacted—sat up, gripped the handle of the knife that was strapped to her ankle, and pulled it free. As Daemon stepped in to kick her again, she swung her arm around and sunk the blade into his thigh. Her attacker's blow connected with little force behind it as his with-knife leg gave out. He went down to one knee, his other leg stretched out, keeping him upright.

Amber withdrew the knife and was on him a moment later, the need to attack like the need to breathe. Her mind flashed with images of her headless brother and her body filled with rage. She saw only red, brought the knife up, let loose a savage cry, and plunged the blade into Daemon's throat. In a frenzied state, she stabbed him over and over, his jugular sliced and spewing. She kept on turning his neck into a pulpy mess until the only thing holding his head to his body were a few strands of stringy meat and the spinal column.

Amber sat atop him, caked in crimson. Her mouth was saturated with his blood, and she welcomed it.

Daemon was dead.

Not satisfied, she chipped away at his spine in ice-pick like fashion until the head finally came free.

Triumph is yours.

With knife in one hand, she curled her slick fingers in his hair, stood and lifted the head high. The jaw hung open as blood trickled to the ground. She screamed in primal rage as she stared at the moon and then heard the cry of another.

Looking, she saw Jade standing a few feet away, gun in hand at her side. The woman's face was a mask of utter terror. She raised her arm and pulled the weapon's trigger.

Click.

Click.

Click.

It was empty.

It's your lucky day.

"He misses you," Amber said and underhand swung the head at her enemy.

Jade let the gun fall from her grasp as she caught the head. She stared at it, seemingly caught in a trance. Amber was already charging and tackled her a moment later. The two collided against the open car door, slamming it shut.

On top of her, Amber said, "You loser scum killed the wrong kid. He was just a boy on his bike. The loveliest boy in the world." With tears falling, she sunk the blade into Jade's chest. "This is for my brother, you evil piece of shit." Amber stared into Jade's eyes. Blood leaked from the killer's mouth as she grinned.

"Fuck—" Jade began when Amber shoved the blade deeper with all her might. Jade never finished her statement as Amber watched the light go out of Jason's killer's eyes.

An uncomfortable stillness filled the air. She sat up and looked around.

It was over.

"It's not fair," she said. "They died too quickly."

I know, but you got them. That's what counts.

"I wanted them to beg for their lives. Then beg for me to kill them. Make them repent." The silence was too much, and Amber screamed until her throat hurt.

You're not done yet.

"I know," she said, then severed Jade's head.

CHAPTER THIRTY-ONE

THE POLICE DISCOVERED THE bodies of Daemon, Jade and Bobby a few days after the fact. An anonymous letter was left in Daemon's vehicle stating how they were the culprits of the murders around town. It explained how they did the killings and what weapons they used. Details were included in the letter that hadn't been made known to the public, ensuring the police that they were indeed the spree murderers and not some roaming cult. The author stated that justice had been served and that no more killings would befall the community, at least none related to the spree murders.

Daemon's and Jade's heads had been found on the hood of the Camry. Jade's vagina had been shoved into Daemon's mouth while Jade's jaw held Daemon's severed penis and balls. Both headless corpses had been left naked on the ground in front of the car with the words *murderers* carved into their backs. Bobby's head was discovered a few feet away in the woods, his body bloated and at the bottom of the pool in his parents' backyard.

The police reported that the bodies found on Bobby's property were of the killers, but they didn't believe it was some vigilante taking the law into his or her own hands. Instead, it was surmised that there was a fourth member. He or she had realized things were getting out of hand and that the police were closing in, and then decided to eliminate any potential liabilities before leaving town.

Though the investigation remained open and nearby towns were alerted to the situation, the town of Spencer, though in shock, was finally able to rest a little easier.

Chapter Thirty-two

Amber recovered at home. She told her parents she'd gone hiking and fallen down a rocky hill. She had been worried they wouldn't believe her. They would see how hurt she was and put two and two together after the police found the bodies. But she quickly realized how ridiculous she was being. They, or anyone else, would never believe she had been responsible, yet alone, even a little involved. Her worry was simply the same guilt complex she'd had as a child, like when she tried pot for the first time and believed with all her heart that her parents would know.

During her recovery, she reflected on everything.

Taking out the murderers did not bring her brother back, but she knew that going in. Her goal wasn't solely about revenge. It was that and more. It was about disposing of human trash and making the world a better place. She became a preventative measure born out of turmoil. She would never be the same Amber again and did not want to be. The Voice was a new ally who would always be there for her and others who needed her, whether they knew it or not.

Before she could help others, though, she needed to take out more trash. When she was ready, she and The Voice were going to return to college and pay Rex, and all who wronged her, a deadly visit.

About the Author

David Bernstein spent twenty years residing in NYC. Missing the countryside, with its chainsaw- wielding maniacs, werewolves and backwoods dwellers, he moved back to Upstate NY where he was raised, and feels much more at home. He spends most of his time with his wife and daughter when not writing, reading, or hiding bodies.

He is the author of Witch Island, The Unhinged, Goblins, The Tree Man, Damaged Souls, Skinner, Relic of Death, The Machines of the Dead Trilogy and more. He loves hearing from his readers.

Acknowledgements

I would like to thank Kristopher Rufty and Candace Nola for bringing this tale back to life. It means a lot that an author such as Krist thought highly enough of my work, and for Candace to want to publish it. As a publisher, Uncomfortably Dark has been an extreme pleasure to work with! They go above and beyond.

A number of years ago, I thanked a number of people in one way or another for the growth of this book. Without going into detail, I want to thank them again: Shane Mckenzie, my Jackpot brother (I hope that tale will see the light of day again!), Matt Worthington, Tristan Thorne, Travis Tarpley, and the great Tod Clark.

And of course, the incredible Sandy Shelonchik and my daughter Summer.

9 798218 374563